About the Author

Rachel Anderson writes, 'I was born into a vast, extended family with aunts, great-aunts, uncles, grandparents, dozens of cousins. So, even when something bad happened, there was always someone to turn to. But I knew that not everybody is so lucky.

After I was grown-up, a boy from a Children's Home came to stay. I hoped it would be for ever. But he hated me, he hated my husband, he loathed our four other children. Most of all, he hated himself. Like Mak in this story, he'd been dumped by his dad, then by his mum, and his grandmother wouldn't have anything to do with him.

He only lived with us for a few months before being moved on somewhere else.

That was twenty years ago. I still think of him every day.

I wish I could have written him a happy ever after.'

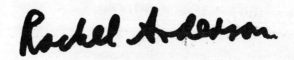

Praise for Rachel Anderson

'. . . there's a personal, original vision here . . . involving and impressive.' Philip Pullman, *The Guardian*

'. . . perceptive writing and quietly provocative approach to themes that are far removed from conventionally acceptable topics for young readers.' Stephanie Nettell, *Books for Keeps*

The Flight of the Emu

Rachel Anderson

Hodder
Children's
Books

A division of Hodder Headline Limited

To Janet O'Hare of Curl Curl Beach, New South Wales

Copyright © 2001 Rachel Anderson

First published in Great Britain in 2001
by Hodder Children's Books

The right of Rachel Anderson to be identified as the Author
of the Work has been asserted by her in accordance with the
Copyright, Designs and Patents Act 1988.

10 9 8 7 6 5 4 3 2 1

A Catalogue record for this book is available from
the British Library

ISBN 0 340 79939 0

Typeset by Avon Dataset Ltd, Bidford-on-Avon, Warks

Printed and bound in Great Britain by
The Guernsey Press Co. Ltd, Channel Isles

Hodder Children's Books
A Division of Hodder Headline Limited
338 Euston Road
London NW1 3BH

Contents

FIRST HOME:
THE BEAUTIFUL VIEWS

Belonging

It was a Friday. You could tell by the smell from the kitchen. Ever since we'd got in from school, Mrs McFee had been busy murdering frozen cod.

Mrs McFee was a lousy cook. But on a Friday she always tried to make us laugh.

Instead of shouting, 'Tea's up!' she seized the potato masher, all sticky with pounded potatoes, held it up to her mouth and began to warble at it as though it was a microphone. We stared. It was like seeing a really bad performer on a television talent show.

'I belong to Glasgy and Glasgy belongs to me!' Mrs McFee sang.

Did she really come from Glasgow? Was that where she'd learned her cookery? I wondered if she knew how to do a deep-fried Mars bar. I'd always wanted to try one. They were invented in Glasgow, so Daniel said.

He'd been an inmate here nearly as long as I had. We slept in the same room. But we hadn't much else in common.

I clapped Mrs McFee.

Daniel shouted, 'Encore,' which means 'More'. (Behind his squinty blue eyes he's a brainbox. He knows the French.)

Aunty Brenda said, 'Oh, I wouldn't know about that. What will you think of next, Mrs McFee!' Aunty Brenda was round and squishy like one of the old armchairs in the Day Room. She had a shiny pink face as though she'd just got out of a hot bath. She liked saying things that didn't mean anything.

We trooped through to the dining-room for our fish and grey-potato-mash tea.

That Friday there was a new child. She was very small and quite young. Aunty Brenda showed her where to sit. You couldn't sit wherever you felt like. You must always sit in the same place at mealtimes. Even in prisons they don't make you do that, so Daniel says. He should know. His dad's in prison.

When she saw the craggy mountain of mashed potato, the new girl looked as though she might cry.

'That's right. A little of what you fancy does you good, dear,' said Aunty Brenda in the soothing voice you'd use to speak to a stray puppy in the street.

'How long am I stopping here, miss?' the little girl asked in a whisper.

'That's not for me to say, is it, flower?' said Aunty Brenda. 'Now you eat up your nice tea and you'll soon find you settle. Bel'Vue's a lovely place. We're all one happy family with never a dull moment.'

You couldn't help feeling sorry for kids when it was their first time and they were finding out about the strange rules.

'They're not rules,' Miss Marshall had told me when I'd complained about having to go up to bed at the same time as Daniel just because we were the same age. 'They're useful suggestions for civilized behaviour to make your collective life here run more smoothly.' Miss Marshall was the manager. She didn't live there but just came by three times a week to do some managing.

'*Bel'Vue* is French. It means "beautiful view". Except it should be spelled "Belle vue". That's what the apostrophe's for, to show something's missing,' Daniel, the know-all, suddenly announced for the benefit of the new girl, even though she looked too young to have concern for the finer points of grammar.

'Some view,' I said.

The house stood opposite the council's Park-and-Ride compound. Every morning we heard the commuters queuing, bumper to bumper, on their way into the car park. On Saturdays, the parking and riding went on all day with the weekend shoppers.

Daniel said, 'It is my belief that the local authority has deliberately sited this children's home near the council's busiest car park as an experiment in cost-cutting.'

Aunty Brenda, who never admitted to knowing anything about anything, said, 'Oh I wouldn't know about that.' She wasn't Daniel's real aunty. She wasn't *anybody's* aunty.

I said to Daniel, 'How will it save them money?'

'The carbon monoxide from the exhaust fumes will poison us. If we're asphyxiated, they won't have to waste money on our upkeep. They'll be able to spend it on useful amenities for the town.'

Aunty Brenda didn't think it was nice to talk about poisoning children. 'Eat up your fish, Danny. You'll only upset the little ones. You know that Bel'Vue's a lovely spacious home. And if you don't like the smell at the front, you can always go out to the garden at the back.'

It wasn't a garden. It was a fenced-in space with black tarmac and three swings.

Perhaps, for Aunty Brenda, Bel'Vue seemed a nice enough place. But she didn't have to be here all the time like we did. She had a proper home of her own where she lived with her dachshund dog and her dippy daughter.

We attacked our cod. Mrs McFee had done a good job. They were definitely dead.

Very occasionally, people from Bel'Vue got away. They got themselves fostered or adopted, or returned to their families. Then there was a farewell party. They could choose their favourite food, like the condemned convict's last supper.

But adoptions didn't happen often. And definitely wouldn't happen to me.

It's very difficult, practically impossible in fact, to get yourself adopted if you haven't first belonged to someone you're still in touch with, so that that person can sign a declaration to say they don't want you any more and won't ever change their minds. Without that document, the lawyers won't do the adoption.

However, sometimes a person doesn't seem to belong to anybody. This is exceedingly rare, but can happen if you're found under a gooseberry bush or in a litter bin, or if the first person you belonged to wanders off without saying where she's going. Then you can't get her signature, which would make you available for someone else to have a turn with you.

Daniel told me that in other countries there are lawyers who'll do anything you ask, even without the

7

right signatures or certificates, provided you bribe them enough. But that wouldn't have helped me because I didn't have any money and I didn't know anybody who might want to adopt me.

Daniel was lucky. He didn't need adopting. He had a mother who said she loved him and saw him twice a year to prove it. He also had a stepfather who hated him and hit him every time he went home. Daniel told me it was important to hang on to anybody, however hard they were, just in case they became useful.

But I was fed up with hanging on. Who'd want to hang on to Aunty Brenda? She was just paid care staff who minded us from Wednesday afternoon till Saturday teatime. From Saturday till Tuesday, we were minded by Aunty Gill (who wasn't anybody's proper aunty, either).

If both of them were ill or took holidays, then we had a man called Kevin with a silver earring. He was a laugh. He let us stay up late and mess around making pancakes, which set off the smoke alarm. Unfortunately, Aunty Brenda and Aunty Gill were hardly ever ill and only went on holiday once a year.

'Goodnight everybody!' called Mrs McFee. 'See you Monday.' She didn't stay to eat with us. She, too, had a proper home of her own. I imagined it stacked up with Mars bars waiting to be drenched in batter and deep–fried in a big pan of sizzling oil. I decided that if I ever

8

got to choose my favourite food for a farewell party, I'd ask for deep-fried Mars bars.

Sharon, who was one of the older girls at Bel'Vue, dissected her fish carefully, then began to push it round her plate.

I said, 'I shouldn't bother. It's too late for it to benefit from regular exercise.'

'Shut it,' said Sharon.

Aunty Brenda said, 'Sharon, dear, it's not for me to say so, but aren't we being a little bitty picky? Shouldn't we give a thought to the starving mites on the other side of the world?'

'Yeah, Sharon, you should count your blessings,' I said. 'Some of those foreign kids are so hungry, they even have to eat the cardboard boxes what they live in.'

'Oh, I wouldn't know about that,' said Aunty Brenda.

'Of course you wouldn't,' I snapped. 'Because you don't know anything, do you, and you've never been anywhere, have you?'

I don't know why I had it in for Aunty Brenda. It wasn't her fault I was living here, any more than it was her fault she was so soft and pink and liked wearing drab cardigans that matched her face.

The new little girl began to sob. 'Home now,' she said. She slid down from her place and tried to snuggle up on to Aunty Brenda's lap.

'No Maisie, petal. I don't think we do that. Not at mealtimes, do we?' said Aunty Brenda. She heaved the child back to her own seat in front of her own cod.

House aunties weren't supposed to show affection for us. That was a rule.

'But why mustn't they?' I'd asked, back in the days when I still wanted to be loved or hugged or touched, even if it was only a quick pat on the head like a dog. Was it in case a member of care staff grew so fond of a particular child that they wanted to take them home? Or in case one of *us* got to like one of *them* too much and cried when they went off-duty?

Miss Marshall soon put me right. 'No, Mak. It is because we don't believe that favouritism is a healthy atmosphere in which to start finding yourself and preparing to move on. It can cause bad feelings. Imagine how you'd feel if I was always taking Daniel out while you were left behind.'

'I'd be glad of the break,' I said.

The new girl, who didn't like her mashed potato, had been brought into care, so Sharon whispered to one of the other older girls, because of abusive parents. That meant she was going to be put through a programme of recovery by social workers, key workers, therapists, counsellors. Poor thing. But at least she'd be safe from harm. Safety, cleanliness and regular feeding. That's what you got at Bel'Vue.

And, by the time you were my age, you were bored out of your brain with it. Cod on Friday. Pizzas on Saturday. Pasta on Sunday. Sausages on Monday.

But then, lo! A miracle. The Tuesday after the new girl arrived (ham, quiche, salad – always cold on a Tuesday so we'd be ready for our weekly House Meeting at 7 pm), something different started to happen, nearly as different as a member of care staff singing into a potato masher.

How to Play Softball

They told the new little girl that Bel'Vue was her home from home. They didn't tell her that it was a dictatorship. Or so Daniel said, and I believed him. Daniel knew about things like that because he had a dad, even if he was in prison.

Miss Marshall, Daniel claimed, was the dictator.

Each week, on Tuesdays at 7 pm, there was House Meeting. Attendance was mandatory, which meant you had to be there whether you wanted to or not. Everybody. Us inmates. Both the house aunties, the stand-by care staff, Kevin, Mrs McFee, the weekend relief cook (but not the cleaning staff, because their opinions were not supposed to matter). As well as any students who'd been loitering around observing us as part of their studies in social work.

And, of course, the dictator herself.

I never saw the point in House Meeting because,

although we were told that we could say what we liked, expressing our views made little difference to how we were treated. Nothing ever got changed. We didn't count as full humans.

On Tuesday afternoon, as soon as I saw Miss Marshall's car drawing up at the front door, I ran out towards it.

'Do I have to come to House Meeting today?' I asked, as she opened her door to get out.

She gave me an acid-drop smile. 'Why? Are you sick?'

'Course not.'

'Then please don't start being awkward. You know House Meeting's important. For the good of everybody. A time to air grievances and iron out hiccups.' She wore a sharp dark suit without a speck or a stain or a dribble on it. Unlike the aunties, she didn't even pretend to like children. She picked up her black brief-case, locked her car, then checked it to make sure. She didn't trust us for a second. I don't know how she'd got the job of managing a children's home. She'd be better at managing things that didn't move or breathe or answer back.

I said, 'My grievance is having to live here in this dictatorship where nobody listens and where my vote is invalid.' (This was something Daniel sometimes said.)

'Then House Meeting is the correct and democratic

13

time to tell us about your troubles. Now run along, because I've got lots of work to do. And if you can't think of anything to amuse yourself with, you can always go and start getting the day room ready.' She took out another set of keys to let herself into the staff office, which was off the hall. She closed the office door quietly but firmly in my face.

I crouched down and called to her through the keyhole. 'I don't know why you've got it in for me. It's not my fault I'm stuck here and don't like it.'

House Meeting took place in the Day Room. It always seemed to be grey in there, even with the lights on. They had weak economy bulbs. The shelves in the Day Room were piled with depressing boxes of Lego, jigsaw puzzles, construction kits, electronic games which either had bits missing or no batteries. People donated old toys when their own children got bored with them.

For House Meeting, the armchairs were pushed back to the walls. We had to sit on the floor in a circle.

Daniel muttered in my ear, 'This isn't a circle. It's more of an amorphous amoeba.'

'A what?' I said.

'The amoeba is one of the lowest forms of living creature. It is single-celled and is constantly changing its shape.'

'Oh,' I said. 'I see.'

Miss Marshall once told Daniel that he knew more words than was good for him. I was glad because that was how I got to know more words.

House Meeting always began with Miss Marshall's throwing-the-softball routine. It was a stupid game. Years ago, one of the social work students had introduced it. She'd called it 'Play therapy'. Now we were stuck with it forever.

Miss Marshall waited till everybody else was gathered in the room before she joined our shapeless circle. People had to shuffle sideways on their bottoms to make room for her and her brief-case. She took the ball from the brief-case and held it up like the Olympic flame for all to see. It was a baby's toy, soft and velvety.

'Hello everybody, and welcome,' she said. 'If you haven't attended before, my name is Miss Marshall. I am currently manager of Bel'Vue residential home and seven other long-stay care centres in the county. Let's begin with the rest of the introductions.'

She tossed the ball into the gathering.

If the ball came your way, you had to catch it and call out your name, then throw it on to someone else. The whole thing was embarrassing and boring and time-wasting. Most of us knew each other's names already. I said it would've been more reasonable for visitors or newcomers to say who they were and for the rest of us to keep quiet.

'Quicker, yes, Mak,' Miss Marshall said. 'But not necessarily so effective as a means of identity affirmation. And that is something from which we can all benefit.'

'Can we?'

'Yes. Knowing who we are is an important stage in our journey towards maturity.'

'Right,' I said with a snort. 'I'll try and remember that.' Not that I believed tossing a velvet ball around once a week was likely to help me know who I was.

The softball landed in front of the new girl, startling her. She recoiled as though a spider had dropped down beside her. She blinked at it, then began to wail. 'Wanna go home. Wanna go home.'

'No you don't!' I said without thinking. If it was true what Sharon had said, why would she want to go back to parents who'd abused her? 'You don't want to go back there!' But whoever they were, they were her family. That was more than I'd got. Bad parents had to be better than no parents. However wicked they were, they gave her a sense of belonging. Like Daniel had told me, people in our situation had to hang on to anything we'd got.

Miss Marshall shot me a stern look. 'Be quiet, Mak, and await your turn.'

The new girl's social worker, who was crouching close beside her like a guard dog, leaned over, picked up the velvet ball, said, 'This is Maisie, and my name is Mandy,' then blushed and threw the ball randomly across the circle. It landed by me.

'Amoeba!' I called defiantly.

Miss Marshall gave me another glare. 'Give your name properly, please.'

'I am. Amoeba means the lowest form of living creature and that's me.'

I chucked the ball to Sharon. At her. I didn't exactly choose her. She happened to glance up and caught my eye. She looked guilty. She was doing homework, learning something, under cover of her sweater sleeves. She annoys me. I admire her too. I suppose she's the nearest I'll ever get to having an older sister. I expect she hates this place as much as I do. Yet she manages to keep her cool, to avoid conflict. I don't know how she does it.

I thought about running away and living rough. But where? This isn't South America. There's laws against kids kipping out on the streets. I looked young for my age. I wouldn't even pass for eleven. I'd soon get picked up and brought back to Bel'Vue, or to another place just like it. In the olden days, they wouldn't have bothered, I could've gone to sea as a cabin boy when it was good to be small. Not any more.

After we'd all done our Identity Affirmation, there was House News. It meant Aunty Brenda or Aunty Gill reminding us of any forthcoming birthdays so we'd know to get cards, telling us if anybody had done anything excellently good at school (very rare), telling us if somebody had nicked something (very frequent) and would they please own up and return the item.

Next came Free Speech, when we were supposed to make our complaints, air our grievances, settle squabbles, say if we wanted to change bedrooms (a request which was always turned down on the grounds that it wasn't convenient that week).

Daniel had been trying to change rooms for months. Finally, he'd come up with his own solution. He'd drawn a black line down the middle of our room.

'My half,' he said. 'Right here. Yours, over there.' He glared at me with his fat blue eyes.

He called his line The Equator.

'What's an equator?'

Even when my questions were really dumb, Daniel didn't mind giving answers. If he ever really got a room of his own he'd miss me, because he'd have nobody to reveal his superior knowledge to.

'The Equator is the imaginary line around the circumference of the Earth that separates the northern hemisphere from the southern hemisphere,' he said.

'Right on,' I said.

'However,' he went on, 'this line here is not imaginary. It is real.'

I was not allowed to step over the Equator on to his side, even though I had to let him come across my bit to reach the door.

It wasn't worth arguing about. He was bound to win because of knowing more words. 'One day,' I muttered, 'one of these days, I'll be away from here so fast you won't see me for smoke, and when I'm gone I shan't be giving you another thought.'

During Free Speech, nobody said anything, except for Maisie, the new girl. She kept up her wail of 'Wanna go home!' Miss Marshall gave a nod and the social worker took her out of the Day Room.

On a whim, I decided it was time to remind Miss Marshall and the aunties about the issue of the duvet covers. I raised my hand to speak.

At Bel'Vue, it was another of the peculiar rules that our duvet covers were colour-coded according to our age. Pink and blue teddies for the nought to five-year-olds. Green trains for five to eights. Red hippos on a blue background for eight to twelves (that was Daniel and me, as well as three girls who giggled a lot). And yellow moons, stars and zodiac signs for thirteens and over.

'Oh please, Mak,' groaned Daniel. 'You're not going to moan about the hippos again, are you?'

'Yes, as a matter of fact I am. She said I'd got to air my grievances.'

It wasn't that I cared two figs about having red hippos the same as Daniel's. It was the being colour-coded that annoyed me. Every coat on its hook. Every child filed away, tidy, silent, under the correctly-coloured bedcover.

Aunty Gill had even told us that her favourite time of day was on night duty when she was doing the late round.

'I see you all tucked into your beds, and sleeping so sound, I get a real happy feeling for you.'

Unconscious, that's how they liked us. Daniel was right.

So my small protest, to prove we could speak as well as breathe quietly, was a matter of principle.

'It's undignified,' I said. 'This regimentation. We shouldn't have to put up with it. We ought to have freedom of choice. I bet they don't do it in proper homes.' Though how should I know? I'd never been inside a proper home, not that I could remember.

Miss Marshall sighed wearily. 'Young man, if it's about the bed-linen yet again, as I've told you before, we'll be getting new supplies when these ones are worn out. In the meantime, how, may I ask, do you achieve such immaculately bad timing? Week after week, you say nothing. This week, when I have an important announcement, which concerns everybody, you decide to hold us all up with your tragic and petty complaints. Could you possibly defer your protest till next week?'

Miss Marshall always claimed her announcements were important, even when they were about something as dreary as not using toilet paper for inappropriate activities.

One of the big girls scowled. 'Oh, let her get on with it, can't you, Mak?' she mouthed. 'Some of us are itching to be out of here and get on with our lives.'

She meant she wanted to go and watch *EastEnders*. She was addicted to the soaps. They all were, the big girls. It was like the telly stars were their real family.

So I ground my back teeth and grumbled about civic rights and how I hadn't got any while Miss Marshall went rabbiting on. If I'd realized the significance of her announcement, that it was eventually going to turn my world completely upside down, and even turn *me* upside down and take me to the other side of the equator (the real one, not Daniel's), then I might have taken a bit more notice.

As it was, I tried to imagine I was an amoeba and could divide myself in two like Daniel said they could. Half of me would sit there in the circle. The other half would get on with its more interesting life, floating freely in warm tropical waters.

Kids, for Sale or Rent

'So, you will be hosting your first ever Bel'Vue Open Day in just ten days' time,' Miss Marshall was saying.

I untangled my mind from my amoeba float. 'Our what?' I said.

'As I have just been explaining, it's when we throw open the doors of Bel'Vue to the general public.'

'Like a fête, you mean? For fund-raising?' There'd been a summer fête at school to make money for sports equipment.

'Mak, I don't believe you have taken in a single word I have been saying.'

'Yes, I have. We're having a fête.'

'No, Mak. We are having an Open Day.'

'What's that?' I had no idea it'd be how I'd get to meet two new mothers.

'Tell him, Daniel.'

'It's so that people can come in and see for themselves

what a warm and friendly household this is.'

I said, 'Why would anyone bother to come up here? Unless they lost their way to the Park-and-Ride.'

'We shall be advertising in the local press and offering tea and cakes.'

Aunty Brenda wanted to know why it had to be so soon. She said she wasn't sure if she could get the house tidied up in time. And that was before she'd discovered Daniel's equator line.

Miss Marshall said, 'We wish Open Day to coincide with the Heritage Festival, when there'll be a celebratory atmosphere all over town. We can all benefit from that.'

Sharon, who didn't usually say much in House Meeting, put up her hand to ask, 'Would you say this is part of some new Social Services fostering campaign?'

'As you know, we've long been concerned with breaking down barriers, dispelling the old myths about disadvantaged children and institutional care. We must forge more strong links between cared-for youngsters, like yourselves, and local townspeople. And, if your Open Day should lead towards the blossoming of a Befriending Situation, between one of you and a member of the public, that would be a useful spin-off benefit.' She was good at words even if she wasn't any good at hugging.

Sharon gave a nod and a grunt. I thought it was a grunt of approval to show she thought it was a good idea. It wasn't till later that I realized it was the opposite.

I went to the kitchen to collect my evening cocoa. Sharon was explaining her disapproval to Daniel.

'It's obvious they're trying some new scam. I just hope it works out and it won't do more harm than good.'

Daniel said, 'How d'you mean? Letting people in to visit can't do any harm, unless they're all axe murderers.'

Sharon told him about something that had happened to her when she'd been younger. 'I was in another home then. The director had this idea how he could get more of us adopted out.'

'Why did he want to do that?'

'Save money, of course, like Daniel was saying the other day. Maintaining kids in care costs. Stands to reason, doesn't it? Once they done their paperwork and paid the lawyers and that, they're shot of you. The new people pay for food, clothes, the lot. So the director's plan was to put us on display in a big department store.'

'What's a department store?'

'Like a shopping mall. Me and three others were chosen because we was best behaved. They did my hair up in bunches with new ribbons so I'd look even younger than what I was. They told me how somewhere out there was the right family for me, all warm and caring. They'd take one look at me and my ribbons, and their hearts would melt. So we was stood there in that store all day with a couple of social workers and a table of leaflets to hand out. From nine in the morning, when it opened, through till closing time. I felt like I was an animal in a pet shop.'

I said, 'If you didn't like being there, why didn't you just walk off?'

'Because back then I wanted it. I wanted a family to want me. I'm telling you, loads of people came up to us. They asked our names. They took the leaflets. Some of them gave us sweets. One old fellow offered us each fifty pence because he thought we were collecting for the home. Like beggars. In a way, we were. Begging for someone to offer us a home, like stray dogs. But of all them hundreds of people who passed by us on that Saturday, not one of them wanted me to go and live with them, did they? Or else I wouldn't be here.'

I said, 'But it was still worth the try, wasn't it?'

Sharon shook her head. 'No way. I've been left with that memory. Standing in that store. Knowing I was a reject. Not just suspecting, but getting the proof of it like that.'

Whatever Sharon felt about Open Day, and even if it

was just another cost-cutting exercise, Daniel and I reckoned it could turn out to be a bit of a laugh.

We both hoped we might get offered sweets or money like Sharon had.

Daniel and I enjoyed getting ready. We painted colourful signs saying 'WAY IN', and 'THIS WAY PLEASE', 'CLOAKROOM', 'GET YOUR TEAS HERE'. On the 'TO THE GENTS' sign, I did a picture of a man sitting on a toilet. Miss Marshall said she'd use all the signs we'd made except that one.

I said, 'That's not fair. What about people who can't read?'

Miss Marshall said sharply, 'I'm sure the dyslexics will have their own means of finding their way around.'

She was still being narky about Daniel's Equator line. She blamed me as much as him. The cleaners spent ages with the Dirt Devils trying to get rid of it. If the Open Day hadn't been happening, she'd probably never have been told about the line.

On the Thursday before Open Day, Mrs McFee got busy baking cakes to offer our visitors. On the Friday, we tidied up the Day Room and Aunty Brenda told us to chuck out any of the jigsaws with missing bits. Upstairs, in our bedrooms, we were allowed to stick up posters on the wardrobe doors. (Not on the walls, because the sticky stuff might spoil the paintwork.)

Daniel put up the two that I'd given him for his last birthday. He'd been really pleased with them. One of them was of a polar bear sitting on the ice in Greenland. The other was of a tall bird with a spiky claw on each foot. It had writing under it that even Daniel couldn't read. He'd had to look it up.

'*Dromaius novaehollandiae* is Latin,' he'd told me. 'And it means "fast-footed Australian".'

He wouldn't have been half as pleased with the posters if he'd watched me nicking them from the posh poster shop in town. That would've made him the knowing receiver of stolen property.

I put up a rude one of two people snogging, but Miss Marshall made me take it down because she said some people might find it offensive.

Not half as offensive as Maisie was becoming.

All the care staff were wondering what to do about her. She wasn't able to start attending her therapy group for another month. Meanwhile, she'd taken to screaming, 'Wanna go home!' at high pitch for an hour at a time. She went red in the face. Her eyes swelled up. Her nose streamed with dribble.

Aunty Gill said, 'The sight of her won't be melting many hearts.'

Aunty Brenda said, 'Come along now, Maisie, don't be a silly-billy. All's well that ends well.'

Aunty Gill said, 'Perhaps it's just her way of expressing herself.'

Sharon, covering her ears with her hands, said, 'Nonsense. Brats like that should be put down at birth.'

Aunty Brenda said, 'Oh, I wouldn't know about that, dear. All life is sacred, isn't it? Well, that's how Miss Marshall puts it.'

Sharon gave one of her dismissive snorts. 'Come off it. Pure rhetoric. Don't talk to *me* about the sanctity of life. Round here, we're all rejects from life.'

Maisie, ignored for a few moments, flung her dish of Rice Krispies across the dining-room.

Sharon was an angrier person inside than she often seemed. Maisie's screaming fits, combined with the plans for Open Day, sparked her off. At evening cocoa time it sometimes tumbled out without her meaning to let it.

'One of my social workers,' she said, 'once told me that being in care has the same effect as having an operation, emotionally. Like, it's a major trauma that affects the rest of your life. But do these people help us cope with it? Flipping heck, no they don't. If an operation goes wrong, like if they chop off the wrong leg, you get compensation for the mistake. But what will I get for spending my life in care and being messed up?'

I said, 'At least you got a room to yourself.'

'Yeah, but what have they *done* for me since I been here? Zilch. Just a constant reminder that I'm one of the leftovers that nobody wants.'

She retreated to her room with her mug of hot cocoa, and slammed the door.

I decided I liked Sharon.

On the Friday evening before Open Day, Kevin brought along some strings of coloured flags. A second-hand car sales place near his flat was throwing them out. He helped Daniel and me to tie them along the chain-link fence. Then we put a huge notice over the front door saying. 'BEL'VUE OPEN DAY. ALL WELCOME. POP IN AND MEET US, 11–4'.

On the morning of Open Day it was raining when Daniel woke me by throwing a trainer at my head. Not just lightly, but heavily. I could hear the swish–swosh–swish of Saturday shoppers driving up the road to the Park-and-Ride and the swish–swoosh of the Park-and-Ride buses transporting them down to the mall, where they'd wander about, in the dry, on the white-tiled walkways, buying things for their homes, clothes for the children, presents for their grannies.

Our first visitor, bang on eleven, was Mrs McFee. She looked different, not wearing her white overall and cap.

'Just popped by to see how you's all doing.'

We gave her a cup of tea and a dainty butterfly cake on a plate. We crowded round while she ate it.

'Och, what fine wee cakes you have here,' she said with a giggle.

The next visitor was Aunty Brenda's daughter, who'd walked up despite the rain to give Aunty Brenda's dachshund some exercise. We made a fuss of the dog and fed it another of the cakes. Then nobody came for several hours, though I saw quite a few passers-by glance over at the bedraggled flags and the big sign saying 'ALL WELCOME'.

The rain kept up all day. Round about half-past three, there was a brief scurry of visitors, real members of the public, wanting to come in and meet us. Miss Cairns should have been among them. She was the first of the women who thought she wanted me. But, since I didn't know that at the time, I didn't miss her.

A man and woman wearing matching navy jogging suits arrived together and stayed longer than most. They wanted to be shown into everybody's rooms.

'I like your animal posters,' the man said to me. He was peering at the *Dromaius novaehollandiae*.

'That one's not an animal. It's a bird called an emu. Can't you see the feathers?' I thought he must be really stupid. Whoever heard of a feathered animal?

'And they're not mine. They're his.' I wouldn't keep stolen property.

'Oh. Well I like them anyway.' He turned to Daniel. 'What's this one?'

So Daniel told him all about the Tasmanian devil, which has such powerful jaws and sharp teeth it can chew right through bone, and eats every part of its prey.

The man in the jogging suit seemed impressed.

Then they admired the painted signs, and the posters we'd put up, and the timetable showing what we were going to have for our tea (pizzas and salad, chocolate pudding).

'That'll be nice for them,' the woman said. 'Seems they feed them well in these places.'

The man played ping-pong with Daniel out in the storeroom where the cash-and-carry foodstuffs were kept. But Daniel was too good for him, so the man only lasted for five minutes before he was out of breath.

As they were leaving, I heard the woman say, 'They're too old, these ones. We're really after a baby. We owe it to ourselves to look for a baby.'

I thought, Yes, Sharon's right. We've been like second-hand goods put on display.

An Hour in Heaven

Open Day was finished. Daniel and I felt flat, like Sharon said we would. Nobody had offered us sweets or tried to give us money.

'Bright faces now, lads. Be Christmas before we know where we are, won't it?' said Aunty Brenda, trying to cheer us before she went off-duty.

Daniel said, 'How can she think it's nearly Christmas? There's another thirteen and a half weeks still to go.'

'I dunno. Perhaps she's really looking forward to it. I bet she has a nice tree.'

We both tried to think what she'd give her sausage dog in its stocking. Daniel's ideas were the rudest.

Then, at ten to five, the last of the visitors turned up. The flags were still drooping along the fence outside, but the sign over the front door had been taken down and the remaining butterfly cakes shared out between us.

She blew in out of the rain and dripped all over the door mat. Her long hair stuck to her neck like silvery cobwebs. She propped her umbrella against the wall, where it made a puddle on the floor and she shook herself like a wet dog.

'Lordy, lordy! What kind of day is this! Not too late, am I? I missed the bus. Shall I take my gumboots off? Would that be all right?' She didn't wait for an answer. She took them off anyway. They were kids' wellies, yellow with green frog faces on the toecaps. Strange boots for a grown-up with grey hair.

'It's supposed to be over at four,' said Daniel. 'And there aren't any cakes left.'

But then Aunty Gill came hurrying through and said, 'Oh hello, you must be Miss Cairns. They're just about to start their evening meal.'

Miss Cairns said, 'No worries. I'll join them. As the uninvited guest.' And she stayed and watched us eating our pizza, which must have been very dull for her apart from when Maisie puked hers up (which was a new trick she did quite often). It was her reaction to Bel'Vue mealtimes. Then Miss Cairns watched me and Charlie clearing up. There was a rota. It was our turn. Charlie was one of the girls, who sniggered and giggled at everything and nothing.

Then Miss Cairns watched me and Charlie set

the breakfast table for the morning. Then she came and sat down in the Day Room and watched telly with all of us. Then it was time for the youngest ones to be taken up to bed. She said, 'Thank you,' to Aunty Gill, put on her frog boots and raincoat and went away.

Daniel reckoned it must have been the most boring Saturday evening of her life.

'Sad case,' he said.

'Yup,' I said.

But she must have enjoyed herself in some strange way we couldn't understand, because the next day, Sunday, she was back. This time she was wearing red leather boots with blue laces and a big gathered skirt. Her long silvery hair was dry and stuck out round her head like a fluffy bush on a snowy day.

She had long ears with droopy earrings hanging from them. Daniel and I told each other they were the longest ears we'd ever seen on a living creature that wasn't a donkey.

She asked if any of us wanted to go out the back and play footie. But nobody did. Probably it was because she looked so strange.

I felt sorry for her. So I said, 'Oh all right then.'

She wasn't very good. It was probably because the flappy skirt got in the way and the earrings kept jangling. I was much better than her. But she didn't mind, even when I told her I didn't think she'd make it into the premiership.

It was a funny first thing to do with the person who might be going to be your mother.

For days, for weeks, for months and years, nothing had happened to me. The next bits of my life happened very fast.

She called back at Bel'Vue specially to see me, even though I'd told her I didn't think she was much good at footie.

'Hello again,' she said, putting out her arm towards me to shake hands. I didn't take it. I did nothing, just stood my ground.

'D'you want to come out for a kick-about?'

I shrugged. 'Dunno,' I said.

'Or we could stay in. Would you prefer that?'

'Depends.'

Aunty Gill was in the hall. 'Oh, do stop your dithering, Mak,' she said. 'Of course you want to go out.' And she practically pushed me through the front door.

We were out for a couple of hours. We went over to the recreation ground. She had a football in a plastic bag. It still had the price sticker on it. She'd bought it specially. But, since she wasn't any use at kicking, we walked about instead. She didn't talk too much. I liked that.

I wasn't unused to going out with women. My social worker, my key worker. When you lived at Bel'Vue, you got to be alone with one of them when they wanted to talk, ask questions, make you speak about yourself. They couldn't bear silences. 'Come along, open up,' they'd say. Always pestering for personal information.

She didn't ask anything. So, after a long time, it was me who asked her a question.

'Why choose me?' I couldn't work it out. Daniel was much better-looking (if you happen to go for round blue eyes like pebbles and yellow hair and smudgy orange freckles like scabs).

She swung the ball inside the plastic bag. She said with a smile that showed all her long yellow teeth, 'You were the one who offered me a piece of your pizza. None of the others did. I was touched by your spirit of generosity.'

'Oh.' I wished Daniel were there, too. He'd have known what to say next.

We reached the far side of the rec. It was getting dark. There were lights beyond the railings. She said, 'Shall we go and have a drink?'

I said, 'There isn't anywhere.'

'Over there.'

It was a pub. I knew it was a pub. It was a grubby place where men spent their giros and pitbulls lounged on the greasy pavement outside. I'd never been in any pub, let alone this one. But Daniel's dad had been arrested in one.

I was shocked and thrilled by her suggestion. There were obviously loads of things about the law and boys in care that this woman didn't know about.

I said quietly, hoping she wouldn't hear, 'There's rules and stuff against that sort of thing.' If only Daniel were here. Afterwards, I remembered one of his good words. Legislations.

She heard. She said, 'Maybe there's a family room. Or we could sit outside in the beer garden.'

It wasn't that kind of pub. But the publican let me come inside and sit on one of the benches at the back, near the Gents'.

'Just don't let the lad jump about,' he said.

Miss Cairns had a glass of beer. She got me ginger beer and crisps. Then dry-roasted peanuts. Then a pickled egg. Then more crisps.

'They don't do food here,' she said. 'Sorrio.' She got more crisps. The best thing of all was she didn't want to talk.

She had pale eyes. They looked right at you in an

interested way. Even when the rest of her wasn't smiling, the sad donkey eyes were. That's why I was beginning to like her.

I looked away in case she thought I was staring. I felt I could trust her, that I could safely tell her a few of the bad things I'd ever done or thought of doing and she wouldn't split on me.

But not yet.

So I watched the men drinking at the bar and the zigzag of coloured lights on the slot machines chasing each other round the screens, and the cigarette smoke wafting up to the ceiling. And I knew my life had begun again where it was meant to.

It was dark as hell by the time she got me back to Bel'Vue. They'd finished their tea and the little ones had already started up for bed. But Aunty Gill didn't say anything about me being back late. That really annoyed me. It was as though she didn't know and she didn't care.

'I've been in the pub,' I said. 'Drinking.'

'Very nice, dear,' she said. 'And don't forget to clean your teeth.'

That was the end of my first visit to heaven.

Daniel said, 'What? You been out with that weird woman who looked like a horse?'

'A horse?'

'Them ears.'

'She does *not*!' What made me say that? I had no need to defend her. I didn't even know her.

I didn't tell Daniel anything more.

'What's she like?' he asked.

I shrugged. 'Dunno.'

'What did you do?'

'Nothing special.'

I wanted to hold it to myself. I went to sleep singing inside my head. If this was what love was about, then I was in love. With a long-eared lady of about a hundred, who had silver hair and wore yellow wellies on wet days and red boots on dry days.

The good feeling didn't last. A day in school washed it away as though it had never been. I got a detention. I don't even know what it was for. By evening I was feeling like a rat who needed something to gnaw.

I spotted Sharon on her own in the dining-room. She was hunched over the table, concentrating. So I went in and picked up the ruler out of her pencil case and drummed it along the radiators. First one, then the next. She took no notice. She had nerves of steel.

I said, 'I thought you had to watch *EastEnders*?'

'I do. But I got to finish this first, haven't I?'

'I don't know. Have you? What is it?'

40

'Homework. If I work, I'll pass the exams. I'm going to go to college.'

'Daniel says any clown can get to college. You just choose dumbo subjects.'

'And after college, then I'm going to university. When I've done that, I'm going to train as a social worker.'

I laughed so hard, with tough false laughter, that I dropped the ruler. But she was serious.

'You're daft,' I said. 'What for?'

She put down her book, which was very thick and had no pictures, and sat back. 'Because, Mak,' she said, 'I have not met a single decent one in six years of living in care. And I want there to be someone for the next generation of fouled-up kids, like Maisie, so they don't end up as fouled-up as us lot.'

That made me annoyed. 'Who're you talking about? *You* may be fouled-up, but *I'm* not.'

'Don't you fool yourself, Mak,' she said. 'You're a really sharp kid, but you can hardly read. You're always nicking things from shops that you don't even need. You're always getting into trouble at school and into arguments here. You never settle to anything. You've got no hobbies or interests. You're like a mosquito buzzing around looking for people to pester. What's all that add up to if it's not fouled-up?'

I was so angry I nearly thumped her. But as my fist

41

went up, Aunty Gill came scurrying into the dining-room with a big brown cardboard box.

'Ah, there we are, just the fellow I was looking for,' she said. 'I need you, Mak, to sort out these Christmas decorations. They're in such a tangle.'

'No way!' I said, and ran upstairs to the bedroom and slammed the door.

I lay on the red hippos seething and sobbing. Not because Sharon was wrong, but because she was almost certainly right. How dare she be right?

I was a fouled-up person. There was nothing I could do to change it. And if Miss Cairns found out, she'd never take me out again.

SECOND HOME:
CHERRY TREE COTTAGE

Like the House that Maisie Drew

There were more shiny days in heaven just ahead. They happened fast, like bright high-speed films. Each time I was back in Bel'Vue, I could rewind and watch them in slow motion many times over.

The very weekend after Open Day, she invited me to her house.

It would be the first time, as far as I remembered, that I'd been inside an ordinary person's house. Boys at school sometimes went round to one another's homes. But no one asked me. I was glad. If they had, they'd have expected me to invite them back to my home, and I'd have had to tell them where I came from.

Mira came to pick me up on Saturday morning. She was my social worker. She wore a huge knitted sweater with coloured Aztec patterns on it.

'Peruvian,' she told me.

She saw me twice a year for the bi-annual Review,

and any time I did something extra-bad at school. But this time it was for something good.

'Makes a change,' said Mira grimly.

I noticed for the first time how she had dark hairs on her lip. Women aren't supposed to have moustaches.

I wanted to visit Miss Cairns on my own. 'You just give me the address, and loan me the bus fare. I bet I can find my own way,' I said. I didn't mean 'loan'. I meant 'give'. A social worker got money from petty cash to pay for all sorts of bits and pieces for a person in care. The amount went up dramatically once you were over thirteen. I couldn't wait. Meantime, she still got something every time she saw me. She was always scribbling figures in her out-of-pocket expenses book.

I went on, 'It'd be cheaper than using up your petrol driving around town.'

I wanted this to be my own adventure. I wanted to keep a friendship to myself for once. It was too valuable to spread it about.

But Mira said she had to do things her way. She insisted she had to drive me there, wherever it was. She told me she had to hand me over in person. She said she had to pick me up again.

'Five o'clock,' she said.

Inside her hot, cramped car, it was like sitting beside a prison escort.

46

'You're still only at the introductory stage of your placement. There are formalities, specially about the first home visit. We must follow correct procedure. You wouldn't want anything to go wrong, would you?'

Of course I wouldn't. So I sat in her car silently, my teeth clenched shut like a dog with rabies.

Whenever Maisie drew a picture of a house (when she wasn't yelling or throwing up or doing some other attention-seeking act), it always looked square and solid and perfect, like a house in a storybook.

And that was just how Miss Cairns's house looked.

I was relieved. After the trip to the dingy Drayman's Arms, I wasn't sure what to expect.

The front had a window each side of the blue door, and two more friendly windows above. The roof was red and pointed. There was a tall red chimney.

Maisie usually put a scribble of smoke coming out of her chimneys. There was no smoke here, though there were flowers in window boxes and a small tree at the front, just as Maisie might have drawn it with her crayons, compact and hung with red and yellow leaves.

Mira went up the path. I followed, dragging my feet. I wanted to be there. I didn't want to. There was a brass doorknocker shaped like a lady's elegant hand. But, before Mira had time to reach for it, the door swung open. And there was Miss Cairns with her wild hair like silver wool, her gaudy gathered patchwork skirt, and her arms powdered white halfway up to the elbows, like a person playing ghosts.

'Welcome, welcome! I saw you coming! Better not shake hands. I'm all floury. I've been making a cherry strudel.'

Mira gave me a shove forward, as if I was a cumbersome parcel to be delivered. 'Here he is,' she said. 'I'll be back for him at five.'

'Bonza,' said Miss Cairns. 'Thanks so much, Miss er-thingo.'

I didn't bother to say goodbye to Mira. I walked straight in through the front door as though I was coming back to my own house. Because I felt that, once I was inside, Mira couldn't get at me again till five o'clock.

'Nice tree,' I said.

'Out front? Yes, isn't it?' said Miss Cairns. 'I grew it from a stone.'

'A stone?' I said. How could anyone grow anything out of a stone, unless they were magic?

'Or should I say "pip"? You know, the tough nut inside the cherry.'

'Oh, a cherry,' I said.

'End of May, that's the best time to be here, when the tree's so heavy with fruit. The birds take a lot away, but they leave plenty for the rest of us. I give away pounds and pounds and I make jam, and pies, and I bottle some. I've even been wondering about trying cherry wine. Oh, I say, do you go a bundle on cherries?'

I shrugged. I had no idea. The only cherries I'd ever eaten were in Mrs McFee's festive fruit salad, which came out of a big catering tin. They were bright pink and didn't have pips or stones inside them.

A tabby cat slid off a kitchen chair, crept towards me, sniffed, then began butting with its nose. I didn't know what it wanted and I felt a bit embarrassed.

'Mr Twitchett apparently approves,' said Miss Cairns. 'Though, if you don't care for cats, give him a push and tell him to go away and mind his own beeswax.'

I had no idea if I liked them or not. I'd never known a cat. At Bel'Vue there weren't pets.

'It is not part of the management policy,' Miss Marshall had said when Daniel tried to bring home a dog he'd found wandering in the Park-and-Ride across the road. 'What would become of the poor defenceless animals if the child was moved on?'

And Aunty Gill had agreed. 'It's hard enough minding you lot without having to go putting up with disturbed dogs into the bargain.'

The tabby went on nuzzling against my legs. I wasn't sure what I was supposed to do.

49

Miss Cairns said, 'You're not allergic to them, are you?'

'I dunno.'

'I don't think you can be. Or they'd have told me. They told me about the other thing.'

I said, 'I don't mind cats, really. Or any animals. I like all animals, I'm sure I do.'

She said, 'I meant the thing about the bed. At night.'

She was on about pissing the bed. They shouldn't have told her. It was personal. An invasion of my civic rights.

'No worries. I've got one of those special undersheets.'

I knew. She meant plastic, which crackled and woke you every time you moved. Daniel didn't have to have one.

'My younger brother went on wetting his bed till he was turned twelve. He was fine.'

How did a woman with snowy white arms and a halo of frizzy silver have a bed-wetting brother?

I said, 'I'm not allowed to stay the night here.'

'I know. Not yet. But when you are. Sorrio I mentioned. The sheet's in place. So as far as I'm concerned, let's regard the issue as *finito, non importante*. I'll show you the layout. Then you can get your bearings.'

The inside of her house surprised me. I don't know what I was expecting. But it wasn't this. Compared to Bel'Vue it was so small. Only two rooms upstairs, two downstairs, and a kitchen not much wider than a cupboard.

'Is that all?' I said.

She laughed. 'There's only ever been me. And Mr Twitchett. But he's somewhat footloose and fancy-free. Goes walkabout whenever the mood takes him. Lives elsewhere half the time.'

Her home was cramfull of stuff, pictures, china toys, strips of coloured cloth pinned up like paintings. The hallway was stacked to the ceiling with books. On every wall in all the other rooms were shelves, and on every shelf were ornaments, pictures, glass beads, wooden boxes, stones, flower vases, decorated china dishes, wooden spoons in jars, pencils, dried seaweed, dead flowers, live flowers. There were books everywhere, even on the stairs and in the bathroom.

I said, 'You got a lot a books here.'

'Have I ever! D'you like reading?'

'Yes.' I don't know why I said that. Maybe I wanted her to like me.

She didn't mind me looking at her stuff, touching things, seeing what they were. She was proud of all her junk.

'That's a piece of sea glass,' she said. It looked like a blue jewel, but I knew it wasn't because she'd explained she didn't have anything that was valuable to anybody else. 'I picked it up off a beach near Curl Curl, that's an unusual place for finding sea glass.'

'Does it grow there?'

'No. They're just fragments of old bottle. They'd have been thrown overboard. Sometimes, a hundred years ago or more. You can tell by the type of glass. Over time, the sharp edges get smoothed out by the movement of the sea.'

I put the blue glass from Curl Curl carefully back in its place. 'Why d'you keep all this clutter? It's not tidy, leaving it about. Miss Marshall wouldn't like it. Everything has to be put away.'

'Blow your Miss Marshall,' said Miss Cairns. 'Do *you* like it?'

'Dunno.'

'So. You don't like it now. Could you nonetheless get accustomed to living with it?'

I didn't know about that, either.

She explained to me about some of the other stuff. Books – who'd given them to her. Stones – why they were special. Every single thing meant something, was a part of her past.

'Am I giving you the gyp? It's just that I know a fair

bit about you. You don't know a thing about me. Somehow, it doesn't seem just.'

I picked up a small grey stone with a twisty pattern on it. 'Is this sea glass?'

'No. That one's a fossil. Sea anemone. I found it in Tasmania. It was already a few million years old. And you're right. I do have a lot of possessions. Too many probably. A person's home becomes a bit like their biography. The older they grow, the longer it gets.'

I didn't know what a biography was. I said, 'I think your gaff's like a museum of jumble.'

She laughed. She laughed at most of the things I said. I didn't understand why. 'You think so? What a delightful notion. The museum of Evelyn Cairns' life. In which case I guess I must be the caretaker, though of course this museum's never open to the hoi polloi.'

'The what?'

'To the public.'

One of the cupboards under the stairs was crammed with a muddle of ancient sports stuff, shin pads, wooden tennis racquets, ski boots.

If she was so sporty, how come she was lousy at football?

'Not mine,' she said. 'My brother's.'

'Why's he keep them here? Doesn't he want them?'

'He's long dead. I don't have living family.'

She pulled out a bat from the cupboard, some stumps and a red leather ball. We went to her back garden to play cricket. Sort of cricket. There wasn't room. She was better at cricket than footie.

'Edward taught me,' she said. 'My brother. He was a real bonzer. Shame you can't meet him.'

She was strange. Women didn't usually have time for cricket. None of the women I'd ever known, anyhow. They were always too busy clearing up, or getting people to therapy on time.

After the cricket, we had food.

She said, 'Just sandwiches. Cheese and tomato. Wasn't sure if you were a veggie. So many are these days.'

'No,' I said, then thought what a good wheeze it'd be to become one. It'd really get up Miss Marshall's nose. She'd have to let Mrs McFee draw up a whole load of new menus, specially for me.

Deep-fried Mars bars. I'd say that's the only kind of protein veggies can eat.

But I wouldn't be staying at Bel'Vue much longer. It probably wasn't worth the hassle.

After the sandwiches, there was the cherry strudel she'd baked. It was a sticky cake thing, with ice cream. She'd made that, too.

After the food, she put on an apron and filled the sink.

I told her, 'We don't do that at Bel'Vue.'

'But you have to help, don't you?'

'Sure. On the rota. But we got a dishwasher. We got to stack it, measure in the powder, set the right programme, switch it on.' Why was I telling her all this? Because I wanted her to know all about me. But the only true things to tell about me were what we did at Bel'Vue.

She said, 'Round here, I'm the dishwasher.'

I said, 'You could have one. You've got space for it, here under the draining-board.'

She said, 'Indeed so. But when would I get the chance to handle my china? Washing it is like being respectful to it.'

Weirdo woman.

'You want to lend a hand?'

'Sure,' I said. What was going on? I was offering to help when it wasn't my turn on the rota. 'There isn't anything else to do, is there?'

'You'll find clean cloths in the drawer. Choose the one you like best.'

The drawers were tidier than her cluttered shelves. The cloths were ironed and folded. The first one I took out was printed with a picture of a curved iron bridge stretching over water that was so blue it was like Maisie had crayoned it.

'Sydney Harbour Bridge,' said Miss Cairns. 'You can

walk over the top. I'd love to try it. Alas, I'd never dare. You have to be roped up. Impressive, isn't it?'

Was it? It looked like a badly printed drying-up cloth. But she must've reckoned it was something special because she said, 'D'you see all the boats and ferries going under?'

I said, 'Yes.'

'They're all souvenirs.' She meant her precious drying-up cloths. 'From round the world, but Australia mostly.'

'Been there, have you?'

'That's where I'm from. A long while back.'

As long ago as a sea anemone fossil?

Another drying-up cloth showed smudgy flowers with writing under each. I didn't try to read the names. I knew I'd say them wrong.

'The indigenous plants of New South Wales,' she said. 'They're so different from the flowers you get here. Sometimes I really miss them, even though I took no notice of them while I was young. D'you know, when I was your age, I *adored* your daffodils, the heralds of spring. Even though I'd never seen one. It was all the fault of that poem we had to learn. D'you have to learn poetry?'

'No.' She obviously didn't know I was in Remedial. 'Not often,' I added.

I chose a cloth showing brown horses with wide fluffy feet pulling an old-fashioned plough across a dreary brown field.

'Ah, the old English shire horses. What an *excellent* choice.'

Congratulated on my choice of drying-up cloth! It was stupid. But it made me feel good, until I realized she'd rather I'd chosen her iron bridge in Australia with all the boats and ferries going under it.

'Don't bother with the plates,' she said. 'They can drip-dry themselves. But the forks and spoons, they'd enjoy it. It makes them feel nurtured.'

When I got back, Daniel kept pestering me.

'What's so special about her gaff? What d'you do over there?'

I'd sorted out drying-up cloths in a kitchen drawer.

I'd played French cricket on a patch of scabby grass.

I'd held a piece of stone that was forty million years old.

How could I tell him? He'd laugh. How could he understand when all he had was an old lag of a dad locked inside a three-metre-wide cell, while I had a new friend who came from the fourth biggest landmass in the world?

He said, 'You going over there for Christmas, too?'

'Dunno. Maybe. It's not up to me.'

'*My* Mum's taking me to Disneyland for Christmas Day.'

I knew he was lying.

'What, at Paris?'

'Nah, the real one. Florida, USA.'

'Nice one,' I said. I didn't bother to let him know I knew he was lying. My dreams were real, not make-believe.

Unbelonging

I went over there the next Saturday, and the one after that.

At Bel'Vue there was never anything to do. At Miss Cairns's, there was nothing to do either and I had to do the nothings her way. But somehow she made even the boring things, like sitting by a fire watching flames, seem interesting.

On the third Saturday something went wrong. I got into an argument with her. I was fiddling around with her bits and pieces while she was outside sweeping up leaves off her scruffy patch of grass. I was inspecting an old-fashioned ink-bottle. I knew that's what it was because she'd told me. It was small and heavy. She'd told me it was made from glazed earthenware and they used to have them in schools a hundred years ago and the ink they used was a black powder which they mixed up with water.

I don't know how she knew all these things.

I wanted to see if there was still any ink left inside, so I tipped the bottle upside down and shook it. But it slipped out of my hand and when it hit the floor it broke into three pieces. There wasn't any ink. It must have dried out years ago. I didn't know what to do. I quickly threw the bits in the bin.

But of course she found them.

'What a pity,' she said.

I mumbled, 'Sorry.'

She didn't seem too bothered. 'Never mind,' she said. 'I expect it had a crack in it already.' She took the pieces out of the bin and put them back on the shelf. 'I'll see if I can glue them together later.'

What made me angry was that she wasn't more upset. 'Don't you even *care* that I've smashed one of your favourite bits of junk?'

'Broken things are a shame,' she said. 'Specially when it's done on purpose. But I'm sure that isn't the case. It's not as though it's a person. Broken people are harder to mend.'

'But it was yours. You told me how you'd found it. Buried in that tip, when you went for that walk, on that day you heard your brother had died.'

She said, 'Nothing belongs to anybody forever, does it?'

I didn't understand. 'Of course things belong to people. Things can't belong to nobody.'

At Bel'Vue the aunties were always going on about what belonged to who. We had to have name-tags on everything that was ours and we weren't meant to borrow other people's things, not even when you urgently needed something like a pair of trainers for school because someone else had nicked yours. Ownership was one of the big conflict points.

I said, 'Cherry Tree Cottage, for instance. It's *your* house. You can't pretend it isn't.'

'Yes, good point. But it's mine only for a while. In another century it'll belong to someone else. A hundred years back, there was someone else living here. A whole family, in fact, according to the deed papers.'

She was difficult to argue with, so I went upstairs to the bedroom that wasn't hers and would probably one day be mine and I sulked for a while. I thought of telling her I wanted to go back to Bel'Vue straight away, just to annoy her. But I realized she'd have said 'Very well' quite calmly.

I didn't want to go back to Bel'Vue ever. I wanted to live here.

When I came down from my sulk, she asked me if I would consider spending Christmas at her house.

'Or perhaps you've already made your plans? I

wouldn't wish to prevent you doing whatever you usually do with your friends.'

I'd said, 'I'll think about it and let you know.' I meant to say, 'Yes', only I didn't want to seem too keen in case it put her off. I didn't want her to know I hadn't got any true friends.

She said that the following Saturday she would be going to London.

'Why?' I was afraid it meant I'd have to stay at Bel'Vue.

'Just for a spot of fun. There's an exhibition I'd like to see. It's about where I come from. My roots.'

She said she'd take me too. She would have to get permission from Mira. I said I thought that was stupid, a person as old as Miss Cairns (she was forty-seven – I knew, because I'd asked her) having to get permission from someone like Mira.

On the train, she unpacked ham and cherry-chutney sandwiches and cherry cake out of her patchwork backpack. She also had some apples, and a dangerously sharp-looking knife with a painted wooden handle.

'Thanks, Miss Cairns,' I said.

'Evelyn,' she said.

I knew it was Evelyn. I'd seen it written.

'You could call me Evelyn if you liked.'

But I couldn't make myself. So I avoided calling her by any name at all, except when I really had to. Then I had to call her 'Excuse me'.

I'd never been to London. I didn't tell her. Maybe she guessed because I was so pleased with everything. London was bustling with pushy people and strutting pigeons. The buses were red, like I'd seen in pictures. Riding on top at the front was like being the pilot of a jumbo jet. I was so excited I couldn't help telling her it was the first time I'd travelled on a double-decker bus.

She raised her eyebrows. 'You surprise me. How do you get around?'

'Walk. School's near. If it's anywhere else, we have to go in the minibus. I hate it. We all do.'

I explained how it had 'Bel'Vue' painted in jolly jigsaw letters on the side with the Social Services phone number so people could tell at a glance we were from some type of institution.

She said, 'I'm a bit of a green person myself.'

'Green?' I said. I thought of her as silvery-grey.

'Inclined towards an ecological and conservationist outlook. Which means I'm in favour of efficient public transport for all. It's not that I can't afford a car. It's the principle of the thing. Would you find it a drag?'

Why was she asking me? At her age, it was her business. If I said I did mind, would she decide not to have me

63

after all? So I said nothing and went on looking out of the window and down on to the heads of people below.

She said, as though thinking aloud, 'Of course we could get hold of a couple of push-bikes, couldn't we?'

My heart gave a jump. I'd always wanted a bike. Everybody my age had bikes – everybody normal. But not at Bel'Vue. Miss Marshall didn't allow them. She said there was nowhere safe to ride. 'Yes, please.'

London wasn't all crowded pavements and pigeons. There were parks too. We could see right into them from the top of our bus. The branches of trees on the edges of the parks scraped along the side of the bus.

From time to time, she pointed out something. 'This is Piccadilly,' she said. Then, 'That's The Albert Memorial. With the Albert Hall opposite. They do concerts. D'you like music?'

'I don't know.'

'I'll bring you some day to one of the Promenade concerts and you can find out. People join in, wear funny hats, let off streamers.'

Sounded weird. Getting bikes would be better.

'We're here,' she said.

We scrambled down the steep steps at the back of the bus and jumped off. The building she led us to had a line of tall flagpoles outside with bright flags flapping. I knew it couldn't be the United Nations building because that's in New York. Daniel told me he was going to visit it when he went to Disneyland.

She said, 'It's called the Commonwealth Institute. So it's concerned with all the countries that are part of the Commonwealth. Australia, New Zealand, Canada and so on. I'm not sure if Australia will be part of it forever. Some of the people want to sever the ties. Mightn't be too bad a thing.'

It was a sort of museum. There was a theatre where they showed films, and a really good café where we had some more food.

It wasn't Disneyland, and I wasn't that interested in knowing how people lived in other countries. Canadian Mounties riding about, Australians hunting kangaroos with throwing-spears, Maoris doing welcome dances, and all that stuff. It was too much about trying to teach you things and pretend it was fun.

But I liked the atmosphere of the place. You could just wander about. I found a table of things you were allowed to touch.

I put my finger on one of them. It was a curved wooden dish.

The guard saw me.

'Yes. Go on,' he said. 'You can pick it up.'

It was only a bit of hollow wood, but somehow I felt scared of it.

He picked it up for me. 'Coolamon,' he said. He pointed to a label stuck on the bottom. He wasn't to know I couldn't read. 'That's what they call them. It was one of their tools. They used them for digging, for carrying food, and for putting their infants in.'

What a horrible thing to do to a baby. I was glad I hadn't touched it.

Then Miss Cairns came and found me.

I said, 'He said those people put their babies into wooden bowls.'

'The first Australians?'

'I dunno. But whoever they were, why would they want to do that?'

'Good question.'

'Was it so they could cook them?'

'No. They weren't cannibals. It was more likely to prevent them crawling away, or to stop the dingoes eating them.'

Miss Cairns wanted to go into the theatre and watch the film that was being shown. So I went with her, just to keep her company. It was a documentary. You could tell it was old because it was in black and white and the picture had spots and squiggles on it. Some men and women were building bungalow houses in the middle of a flat bleak landscape.

'Those people are like my grandparents,' she

whispered. 'It's Tassie. That's where I originate from. Or my folks do. It's an island.'

Obviously it couldn't be anything like the Isle of Wight where Aunty Brenda went on holiday with her daughter and her dog, because Miss Cairns wasn't anything like Aunty Brenda.

'Tasmania's on the other side of the world. My grandparents sailed there on a ship from Southampton. They arrived with nothing except their dreams and the government grant, and after a year they set to and built their own house. Then they had my mum. And when she grew up, she sailed to Australia and had my brother and me. When I grew up I came to Britain. Now there's only me left. Funny old world.'

I said, 'You've got Mr Twitchett, too.'

'Do I ever!'

The trip was obviously important to her. I suppose I enjoyed it because she did.

Of course, Daniel asked me where I'd been, what I'd done.

I said, 'I was finding out how the first Australians made fire with a boomerang and some softwood. Fire was their best thing. It kept evil spirits out of their camp.'

He looked at me blankly. 'You what?' he said.

67

I was pleased. At last, I was able to know something that he didn't.

By my fourth visit, Miss Cairns began doing more talking, asking more questions. I didn't like that so much.

'They say you're quite a bad lad,' she said.

I thought, *Who* says? I could bet it was Mira. 'I'm not that bad,' I said. 'If I was that bad, they'd have sent me off to reform, or to one of those wilderness camp places.'

'*I* don't believe you're a ratbag. You're probably not all innocence, either. But I believe you've probably had a raw deal. If I can do anything to put it right before it's too late for you, then I'd like to give it a whirl. What d'you say?'

'What?'

'I guess this is a bit like a proposal. Maybe it shouldn't be this way round, me asking you.'

My heart was thumping even more than it thumped thinking about the bicycles.

'I've already had all the meetings with the social workers. Yours and mine.'

'Yours?' I thought only bad children had social workers.

'They've appointed the guardian *ad litem* for you. And they've done the assessment.'

I felt panicky. I didn't like it. It felt like I was drowning and couldn't breathe. 'What assessment?' If I had to be assessed, I'd never pass. 'I can't do tests. I told you.'

She laughed. 'Not you. Me. I had to be assessed. The home study or whatever they call it. That's what the social worker was for. To make sure I'm not some clapped-out old drongo. And she's done it and written it up and presented it to the panel. Sniffed into every corner of my life. Turned me inside and out. Quite an ordeal that was.'

The panic faded. It was going to be all right.

'Thank you, Miss um, um, Evelyn,' I said.

She smiled from one long ear across to the other ear. I could see she wanted to give me a big friendly hug. But I wasn't ready for that sort of yuk yet. Perhaps I never would be. But I stuck out my hand towards her. Hers was cold and dry, but firm. We shook hands. It wasn't a proposal. It was more like a seal of agreement.

'Blood brothers,' I said. 'We ought to use that knife you got, make nicks in our skin, make it bleed, then rub them together.'

She said, 'I don't think I'm up for that. But we could drink to it. If only I'd made that cherry wine. Perhaps a pot of tea would do.'

But then Mira arrived.

'Hello there, Evelyn,' she said to Miss Cairns. 'Hi

69

Mak,' she said to me. 'Time to go home now.'

Back to the place that wouldn't be my home for much longer.

After that, things should've been sorted quickly, like Miss Cairns said they would. Mira said so, too. A bit more paperwork. Then we'd go to the Magistrates' court and stand in front of the magistrate and he'd ask me if I wanted to be adopted by Evelyn Cairns and I'd say, 'Yes, I do.' And I'd have to say it loudly and clearly so there'd be no mistake, for my reply would be like my promise, my bond. Then the adult people would have to sign the bits of paper and that'd be it. Miss Cairns and I would suddenly become a mother and her son.

I told Daniel about it because he was interested. He was thinking of becoming a lawyer when he grew up so he could get his dad out of prison.

He said, 'You'll have to stop calling her "Miss Cairns". You'll have to start calling her "Mum".'

I said, 'No, I won't be doing that. I'm going to call her Evelyn. We've agreed.'

Daniel was impressed. 'My mum's name's Jade. Maybe I'll call her that.'

And all these beautiful things should've happened. But life's not a fairytale. Nobody lived happily ever after because getting to belong to someone is never as easy as it looks.

The Slimy Pit

I'd seen Evelyn every Saturday since Open Day.

Then, suddenly, the visits stopped. Just like that. Mira showed up at Bel'Vue on Thursday evening to tell me she wouldn't be driving me to Cherry Tree Cottage on Saturday morning.

I said, 'But she's expecting me! We've got plans.'

We were going to look at second-hand bikes at a street market she knew of. Then we were going to make mincemeat for Christmas mince pies, with raisins and apples, preserved cherries, suet, spices and a measure of Jamaican rum.

'I think not,' said Mira, through her thin lips.

The hall at Bel'Vue is usually a greyish colour. All at once, it glowed with a strange and scary hot red which made me very upset, so that my fist went up.

'Now, don't you go getting in a paddy with me, young man,' said Mira, catching hold of my arm before it came

71

into her face. 'Specially not when I've had the decency to come here outside of my working hours to tell you in person. I thought you'd prefer it to a phone message. You might show some gratitude for all I've been doing for you.'

I thought of the word that Daniel had taught me, for a female dog. I said it to her.

'Bitch. That's what you are. You've done nothing. Bitch. Bitch.'

You're not supposed to swear at your social workers or try to attack them. For a young woman, Mira was surprisingly strong. For my sake as well as hers, it was just as well I didn't manage to hurt her. It would have turned out a lot worse if I had. She got me in a firm grip and led me up to my room.

'And you'll come down when you're in a fit mood to be in the company of other children,' she said.

Later, when she'd gone and I'd calmed down and had my Final Conduct Warning from Miss Marshall, I asked Aunty Brenda why I wasn't allowed to go to Cherry Tree Cottage any more.

'It's not for me to say, is it?' she said, which meant that she hadn't a clue. She was just a weary care worker in a drab cardigan, not a trained social worker.

On Saturday, I gave Maisie some paper and crayons and got her to draw one of her house pictures. Square with a window either side of the blue door, and two windows above, with the pointed red-tiled roof, the brick chimney and the little tree in front like a lollipop.

I wrote 'Cherry Tree Cottage' under it and I stuck it on the wall by my bed and lay there all through Saturday afternoon looking at it and wondering what Evelyn Cairns was doing.

As soon as Aunty Gill came on duty at teatime, I tried asking her why I hadn't been allowed to go. She said she didn't know. 'But I'm sure someone will have made a decision in your best interests.'

What had I done? What had Evelyn done?

Daniel wasn't any help, either. 'I knew it wouldn't work out for you,' he said. He wasn't smiling, but I could tell he was pleased it hadn't. 'I had an intuition.'

I didn't bother to ask him about intuition.

I remembered Sharon once saying how she didn't really know how people like us, who weren't even criminals, got to be put in children's homes in the first place.

At least she'd worked out a way to escape. She was educating herself into a different life. But she was older than me, and cleverer.

'You could try really hard at school, Mak. I'd help. It's not too late,' Sharon said.

'Yes, it is.'

For me, there was no way out of this place. It was a deep slimy pit. Just when I thought I'd clawed my way to the top and could see the faraway horizons shimmering blue, I'd lost my footing and been sent slithering back to the bottom. I was trapped down here till the day I was eighteen, when they'd give me my National Insurance card, a lodging voucher, and the address of a crummy bedsit on the edge of town.

A new social worker came to see me. She told me that Mira had gone off to have her baby.

What baby? I wanted to ask. I hadn't even noticed she was pregnant. It must have been hiding inside the big Peruvian sweater. I was glad I hadn't hit her.

The new social worker was full of enthusiasm and told me her name. I didn't bother to remember it, though I remembered she had a big chin. At least she didn't have a moustache.

'We know how disappointed you must be,' she said. 'However, when one door closes, another always opens. I'm going to push my hardest for you. And that's a promise. Try and think of me as your friend, won't you, and let's see how it goes.'

But she, no more than the others, could tell me what had gone wrong.

'I'm afraid I really don't know. Your case notes aren't

up to date. It was probably just one of those things and you've got to accept it.'

One of what things? Did that mean it was my fault? Or was it Evelyn's? I went through it again and again in my head.

'Though I dare say it brings back all your negative feeings about Maureen,' the social worker said. 'That's only natural.'

'Maureen?'

'Your birth mother.'

'Oh. Her.' She was the one who dumped me.

'Yours is a highly interesting case,' said the social worker. 'I'm really getting into it.'

I guessed why she thought I was interesting. She'd been through my case notes and found out about the tiny bit of Chinese. Mira had been interested in that, too. I remembered her saying, 'You know, Mak, with your looks you could almost be a Peruvian. They're wonderful people.' Mira had got it wrong first time.

It didn't matter to me. I already knew about it. I'd been told. 'There's a bit of the eastern promise in you. On your father's side. The thieving dog. Not mine.'

That's where I'd got my name. From him.

The new social worker with the big chin was eager to go through my Life Book with me. They were kept in the metal filing cabinet in the office. We each had one.

When she found mine, she didn't think there was enough in it.

'Jeepers, it's only half completed. She should have had this finished by now. What was your key worker up to? She was supposed to be your enabler.'

I said, 'Not much has happened to me.'

'You've still had a valid life. It should be respected. Only the best should be good enough for children. Children are our nation's future.'

The Life Books were scrapbooks. Somebody was meant to help you find suitable things to stick in, and write captions and dates underneath. Then, wherever you got sent, whatever happened to you, even if you got brain damage or Alzheimer's and lost your memory, you'd always have the Life Book to remind you of your past and who you were.

You would turn the pages and look at the used video card stuck in, the postcard a long-ago social worker had sent you from her holiday in Mexico, the gift tag off a birthday present from Mrs McFee, the fifty-metres swimming certificate you'd won at school. Daniel had loads of stuff in his. His dad sent him things.

Mira had said you weren't supposed to put in bad things, like Detentions, and warnings about aggressive incidents towards staff, even though they might be an important part of your life.

If you were lucky enough to have a birth certificate they'd let you look at it, but not keep it.

'That's an important legal document. It has to be stored in a secure place. What if you lost it?' Mira had said as though the certificate which said that I was me was a whole heap more valuable than the body that was me.

She'd made me a blurry grey-and-white photocopy which reminded me that my biological mother's name was Maureen, that I was born in Cardiff, Wales, that Dr Patel, MD was in attendance, and that it had been ten minutes past eight in the morning.

The biological father wasn't mentioned, but I knew he was a merchant seaman with a bit of foreign blood in him and that after a few months Maureen had changed her mind about him and decided she didn't like him being around after all.

She must have been a consistent person, for a year on she'd decided the same about me.

The social worker, whose name I couldn't remember, said in a gentle voice, 'The "birth" mother, we usually say. Rather than "biological". It sounds more friendly. Would you like to talk about her?'

I wanted to talk about the other almost-mother,

Evelyn. About her cluttered house, about how there were small lace mats everywhere, underneath every vase, china ornament, wooden carving.

'Doilies, they're called,' Evelyn had told me. 'Silly, aren't they? But I get a great kick out of these old-fashioned things. My Tasmanian granny used to make them. She was a sturdy working woman, with big red hands. Making dainty mats was her hold on gentility. She tried to teach me. But I was impatient. Now I wished I'd learned. Another ancient skill lost to time.'

I'm glad I didn't say anything to the chinny social worker. I'm glad I kept Evelyn to myself. She'd have shifted my words into something different, the same way she'd been updating my case notes.

On one of her visits, she handed me a sheet of typed paper. 'I've been writing a description of you,' she said. 'It's what's called a thumbnail sketch. I have to get your approval. So say if there's anything you don't like.'

I pretended to read it to myself, then let her read it out loud.

' "A lively and imaginative boy, with an endearing personality and a cheeky grin. After a troubled start, Mak is now yearning for a taste of family life. Good at woodwork and sport, enjoys helping around the house. Small for his years, but self-reliant." '

I told her it didn't sound like me at all.

She said, 'Well, I thought, "Let's wipe the slate clean for him. Then at least he'll stand a fighting chance." '

It sounded to me like telling fibs.

'There's no need to go putting people off at the first hurdle, is there?'

'I'm not a horse in a race,' I said.

'D'you want to hear the rest?'

'OK.'

' "An adoption allowance may be payable." '

I interrupted her. 'What's that mean?'

'Exactly what it says.'

'I thought you said you were going to find me ordinary normal parents. Not people who have to be bribed to have me. Aunty Brenda says there's people who adopt children out of the goodness of their hearts. I think you should cut that bit out.'

'No, I have to put it in.'

When she started reading again, I pretended not to listen. ' "He has a Statement of Educational Needs and receives additional support within the mainstream school." '

I didn't need to ask what that meant. I knew. Remedial dumbo.

' "He is subject to a full Care Order and needs a one- or two-parent family where he would be the only child, or the youngest by a significant margin. He would like to be able to keep a pet, preferably a dog." '

'Who put that in?'

'I did. People like dogs. "We would welcome enquiries from across the country." '

I thought, No, we wouldn't. I didn't want to move across the country or I might never get back to Cherry Tree Cottage.

Eventually, she sorted out the thumbnail sketch to her satisfaction and she went away.

Over in the Day Room, everybody was busy being helped to send Bel'Vue greetings cards to their family or friends. So I sent one to Evelyn. Inside it I wrote, 'Please writ to me as soon as posibble as I wuld like to speak with you. This is importat. Your's sinserelly and happy Christmas.'

I wasn't too hot on the writing. I knew I should've got Daniel to help. I posted the card and waited and waited for the reply. The card got sent back to me. It had Post Office writing on the envelope. This time, I did have to get Daniel's help.

' "Return to sender," ' he read. ' "Address insufficient." You great wally! You should've put the street name and the postcode.'

So I bunked off school next day and went to look for Cherry Tree Cottage. I wished I'd paid more attention when I'd been whizzing along in Mira's car.

I walked till my legs ached. I found loads of streets that looked nearly right. I kept thinking I was there. And then I wasn't. It was already dusk. There was a cold clammy smell in the air. I was on my way back towards the last roundabout before the long road with the Park-and-Ride at the end of it when I recognized the turning I needed. Evelyn's cottage had always seemed to be away from town, out into the countryside. In fact, it was nearer than I'd realized. With two bikes it would've been so easy for us to go just about anywhere we wanted.

There were streetlights, but no light in her house. It didn't look abandoned, just as though nobody was there. Mr Twitchett wasn't about, though I called for him. The leaves had dropped off the cherry tree. Its trunk and branches were black, which made it look dead though I knew of course that it wasn't. It was just winter.

I tore a page out the back of my geography book and wrote a note.

Dear Evelyn, To wish you a Mery Christmas wherver you may be. I wuld like to see you agin if I can. What it was I have done wrong, I am sory. If I was rude or whatever. Or have you gone to live in anoter place? I still wuld like to see you agin. Or heaere from you. Yr's, Mak.

I pushed it through the letterbox and made my way back to Bel'Vue. Aunty Brenda was in a flap with me for being so late that I'd missed tea. (Spaghetti tuna bake and sweetcorn.)

I told her I'd had a Detention.

'Well, fancy that! The things you get up to,' she said. 'But it's not right, is it?' she added, which meant either that she believed me or that she wasn't listening. 'Shall I do you an egg? We're all at sixes and sevens round here. That's Christmas for you, isn't it? I suppose I'd better.'

So I spent Christmas at Bel'Vue, same as usual. Same Christmas pudding made by Mrs McFee, looking like black rock and tasting like tar. Same useless stuff in stockings. Same presents from care staff to us (music cassettes, jokey seasonal socks with winking reindeer noses). Same presents from us to them (cheap disgusting chocolates, cheap bath oil). Same plastic Santa stuck on the dining-room door. Same carol singing. Same hours and hours watching telly in the Day Room.

On Christmas Eve, Daniel went over to his mum's and came back on Boxing Day with a sack of presents and a black eye.

In February I got to meet my new parents.

'They're both terrific fun. Very young at heart,' said

the social worker. 'I'm sure you'll all get on like a house on fire. It'll be long-term fostering with a view to permanency. That's what you want, isn't it? You deserve the best. So let's see how it goes, eh?'

The day they came to collect me I recognized them at once. They were the couple in slippery jogging suits who'd come on Open Day and played ping-pong with Daniel and said they really wanted a baby.

THIRD HOME:
57 SOUTHDOWN AVENUE

Reserved Seats

There was a farewell party (the usual) for the condemned person. But no deep-fried Mars bars, because Aunty Brenda said, 'Oh dearie me, whatever next! I wouldn't know about that!'

Instead, Mrs McFee baked a farewell cake. It had 'Bon voyage' in yellow sugar icing on top.

'That means, "Have a good trip",' Daniel told me, and everybody else, in a loud voice.

'As if I didn't know,' I muttered.

'Don't you *want* to go?' he asked.

I'd always been keen to get out of Bel'Vue. But in my own time. I didn't rate the speedy way it was happening. I felt I was being pushed.

The couple were still wearing their blue jogging suits when they came to pick me up. If I'd had the chance to choose the dad of my dreams, it wouldn't have been him. He was a bearded slob with a round belly under his track-suit top. He had greasy hair tied back in a ponytail.

She kept fussing with her earrings and checking the time on her watch. It was gold. Daniel said he didn't think it was real.

They were called Robert and Gwendoline.

'Call me Wendy,' she said, putting her arm round me and giving me a squeeze. 'And he's Bob.'

The fat-bellied slob grinned.

We were going to go to their place by train. It wasn't far.

At the station, Wendy said, nervously, 'I expect you're accustomed to travelling everywhere by car?'

'No. Not specially.'

'We used to have a car,' she said. 'Until quite recently.'

'It wasn't really ours,' said Bob.

Wendy said, 'No, it was a company car. Bob lost it when he was made redundant. He didn't get much of a redundancy pay-out either, did you Bob? It wasn't fair.'

That was the first time she whined about money. Right then I didn't know anything about redundancy pay-outs, so I just nodded and said, 'Oh.'

'Take a good look at the station,' said Bob. 'Memorize it.'

It looked like the train station. It was the station. I'd been to it with Evelyn when we went to London.

'And watch out exactly how we go,' said Wendy. 'Because this is the way you'll be coming to school.'

It was the start of half-term. The train was crowded out with noisy kids and families.

'Our places are prebooked,' said Wendy. 'I knew it'd be safer. It's not far but we didn't want you to have to stand.'

We had to shuffle along the narrow aisle between the rows of seats till we found the right ones. They were in a foursome, two facing two. There were white cards stuck in the top of each place. Wendy checked them against the tickets. They put me next to the window.

'So you can see out,' said Wendy. 'Though I dare say you'll get sick of the view once you start doing it twice a day.'

I thought, How does she know what I'll get sick of? She knew next to nothing about me.

Wendy sat herself down beside me, much too close. I could feel her thighs through her shiny blue jogging trousers. Bob sat opposite, facing me. His knees were nearly touching mine.

Wendy said, 'Are you hungry? I'm afraid I didn't think to bring any picnic. It's only three stops down the line. But Bob could pop along and purchase you a burger from the buffet if you like?'

I shook my head. I didn't feel hungry. I felt like my stomach was full up with cold custard. I don't usually feel sick. It was her mentioning being sick of the view that brought it on.

An old woman came and sat in the fourth seat, facing Wendy.

'Well, aren't we snug?' said Bob.

I shifted myself to the furthest edge of my seat to leave a gap between my elbow and Wendy's. I didn't want the old lady to think we were connected.

But when the inspector came down the carriage stamping tickets and smiling at everybody as though it was his half-term, too, Wendy flashed out a Family Railcard so there was no way of pretending I wasn't with them.

What right did she have to go buying a Family Railcard before I'd properly moved in with them?

'Marvellous, aren't they?' said the old woman, nodding at the Railcard. 'My daughter's got one too. Saves her pounds and pounds whenever she comes over with the grandchildren.'

Wendy said, 'Ours is brand-new.' She glanced proudly at me and patted my arm to show her ownership. 'It's the first time we've ever used it.' I thought she was going to tell the woman that I was brand-new too, and that she'd just picked me up from the showroom.

I got up. ' 'Scuse me,' I said. I edged past their knees.

'All right?' said Bob with an encouraging grin.

Of course I wasn't all right. I was stuck on a train with them, and all these other strangers, heading for destinations unknown.

'I think you'll find it's that way,' said Wendy, nodding her head towards the far end of the carriage, then silently mouthing 'Needs the toilet' at her husband.

That's right. Let everybody know I'm looking for the bogs.

'Oh,' I said. 'Right.' As though I couldn't read the sign.

I didn't really need to go. I had to get away from the cosy foursome. I made my way to the end of the carriage and peeked in the toilet door. I wouldn't have gone in that toilet even if the Mafia were right behind me. It smelled. The walls were damp. The floor was wet with something.

Back at Bel'Vue the toilets were always clean. Aunty Brenda said, 'You can't go far wrong in life if you know how to keep a clean toilet.'

I propped myself against the wall by the train door. It's supposed to be dangerous, in case the door suddenly swings open. Then you'll be sucked out by a rush of air on to the line. If that doesn't kill you, then the train coming along in the other direction will. So what? At least I wouldn't have to sit with them.

A squaddie was travelling there too, in that non-place between compartments. He was sitting on his kit-bag. There weren't any empty seats left on the train. He looked as though he preferred sitting there, content and confident. Short cropped hair, tanned neck, strong arms, pink sunburned ears. Perhaps that's what I should do as soon as I could get away from being in care. Join the army and see the world. Or the French Foreign Legion. That'd get me away. To a desert with kepi caps and camels, except I'd have to learn French.

I was going to ask the soldier how old you had to be to join up, and how you went about it, but the train began slowing. Bob appeared through the sliding glass door.

'Next stop's us,' he said with his encouraging grin.

I felt a lurch in my stomach as though the custard was moving upwards.

Wendy was right behind him. 'Ah, there you are. We were just wondering. Thought we might have lost you.'

When the train stopped we'd have to get out, and go to their house, just the three of us. Nobody else.

I wanted to stay on the train. Go with it wherever it was going. Seek my fortune in a strange town at the end of the line.

57 Southdown Avenue was a four-bedroomed house with just them in it. And now them and me.

'Plenty of room for all of us,' said Bob.

They didn't have knick-knacks, or old ink jars, books, pebbles. They had swirly carpets and swirly wallpaper and swirly curtains. Everything matched.

Almost before I'd sat down in their swirly orange and brown sitting-room, she was telling me to move.

'Mind your feet on the covers,' she said. Then, 'Oops! There I go again, silly old me. Shouldn't have said that, should I?'

Bob smiled at her, then winked at me. 'You can tell she's a houseproud woman, can't you? You and I, we'll have to watch it with our big feet.'

I shifted quickly, stood up and looked at the wallpaper. But you can't admire swirls for long, not if they're all the same.

She said, 'This is your home now, not just mine. I'll have to remember that. And boys will be boys. Only I just thought how a nice boy like you wouldn't want to go putting your trainers on the settee covers, not if you'd realized they'd just come back from the dry-cleaners.'

'She's had it all spruced up in your honour,' said Bob. He rubbed his roll of belly and gazed at her as though he wished the clean-up had been in his honour.

I wondered where she meant me to sit if I wasn't supposed to sit on the armchairs.

I remembered Daniel's advice. 'Whatever happens, get them before they get you.' I hadn't been sure what he meant. Now I knew. I must be on my guard all the time. I had to keep one step ahead, preferably two.

Home Sweet Home

I sat myself firmly on the floor, cross-legged on the swirly carpet.

'Oh no, you shouldn't be putting yourself down there, dear,' she said. 'You make yourself comfy.'

'This is fine. I like the floor.' The squaddie on the train had sat on the floor. He'd looked happy. Perhaps he'd been going home on leave to see his mum.

Bob said, 'Time for a cuppa!' and went off to make it.

She sat on her dry-cleaned settee. Occasionally, she glanced at me and moved her lips into the shape of a smile. It was like she was admiring her new purchase, and patting herself on the back for getting a bargain.

Bob came back with three cups of tea.

'Saucers, Bob!' Wendy said.

Bob went away with the cups of tea, and came back

with them on a tray with three saucers. He handed one to me.

'Sugar?'

'No,' I said. 'Don't drink tea.'

'Coffee?'

'No.'

'A soft drink, then? Squash? You must be thirsty after the journey.'

'I'll get a drink of water from the tap later on,' I said.

They were bug-eyed. I was glad. Perhaps they thought I was going to dehydrate and curl up like a desiccated amoeba on their swirly carpet. Amoebas can only flourish in a watery environment.

They slurped their tea quickly. Bob said, 'Would you like to see your room? Wendy's been decorating it for you. She's done it ever so nicely.'

Wendy nodded. 'Strong masculine colours.'

He said, 'The social worker saw it and said it's as good as a professional job. Are you sure you don't want to come up and unpack?'

'Put your things in place?' said Wendy, in case I didn't know what 'unpack' meant.

'No, thanks. I'm fine here.'

That unsettled them. That I'd sat down and wasn't going to budge till I felt like it.

When they went off to see about making a meal, I

played about with their TV. It was massive. Took up most of the window-bay. They had zillions of videos. I looked through them. It was all recordings of soaps and sitcoms. There weren't any decent films. So I flicked through the channels. It was good having a telly to myself, not having Maisie and Daniel and Sharon and all the rest of them fighting over what we watched. Funny thing was, after a while, I sort of wished they *were* there, all noisy round me, trying to grab the remote control out of my hand, all of us switching channels like we were watching fireworks. That's what I was used to. Never getting to see any programme right through.

At bedtime, they both said goodnight to me. But she went further than that. She tried to give me a hug. The custard feeling came on me again.

Bob rescued me.

'Hey, easy now, Wendy,' he said. 'Maybe he doesn't like the touchy-feely stuff. Save that for me.'

Dead right, old man, I thought.

Bob gave me one of his big winks.

Within a week I'd managed to draw an imaginary black Equator circle round me. It moved with me. They couldn't see it. I could. All the time. It protected me. If one of them stepped over that line into my space, I was able to step back into my own hemisphere.

It wasn't that I didn't like them. They were probably OK. I had nothing to compare them to. I'd never lived with two adults, one male, one female, who were trying to be parents. Any more than they'd ever lived with anyone like me.

So they weren't that bad. Specially Bob. He was quite a laugh if you liked bearded slobs with lank hair who kept winking. And he did a wicked take-off of my social worker.

'Guess who? Guess who?' he'd say, striding into the sitting-room with his barrel chest stuck out above his roll of belly. 'That's it! You've got it! Our best friend, Miss She-Who-Shall-Be-Nameless!'

Made me laugh out loud.

But one laugh wasn't enough to keep me there. The whole arrangement was wrong. I wasn't meant to be there. I knew I was meant to be with Evelyn at Cherry Tree Cottage. I had what Daniel used to call an intuition. A sort of feeling that was so strong it began to feel real.

I went through every conversation with her I could remember us having. The one I liked best was on the last Saturday I'd been over there, except I wasn't to know it was going to be the last. We'd made up the fire in her front parlour with twigs and fir-cones we'd picked up in the park. We were toasting teacakes on the end of sticks even though she had an ordinary electric toaster in her kitchen.

But she said, 'We'll not bother with that. Let's be like swagmen round our campfire in the outback.'

The teacakes tasted burned and smoky. We smothered them in cherry jam.

She got talking about the seaside. She asked if I'd ever been. I said I had once. Then she talked about the oceans around the world. She knew all their names. North Sea, Mediterranean Sea, Atlantic Ocean, Pacific Ocean, South China Sea. She said that, overall, there was more sea than there was land. Good for amoebas, I thought.

Then she said something really strange, to do with me coming to live with her. She said, 'You could say I've been waiting all my life for whoever the sea would wash up. I made myself available. I stood on the shore and waited and you were the one.'

I wasn't sure I liked being a bit of seaweed in her life. I said, 'Yeah, and when something's washed up by the sea, sometimes a big wave comes along and snatches it back.'

'That's a risk I'll have to take.'

'Or else it's the other way round,' I said. 'And the people on the beach don't like what they got and toss it back into the water.'

Evelyn said, 'Well yes, indeed. I suppose I *might*. It's pot luck, what you get, just like for any parent. They might not like the child who was born to them. They might want to toss that back.'

I said, 'Just like the biological mother did to me.'

Evelyn half nodded and the long earrings jangled. 'I know. And I'm sorry.' She put another handful of fir-cones in the fire. They sizzled and flared.

'That's the resin in them,' she said.

I said, 'And what if the bit of seaweed what's got washed into your life changed its mind after a bit and didn't want to stay?'

'Fair enough. That'd be the seaweed's prerogative. You're the child, I'm the adult. I would be very, very sad. And I'd like to think, I'm hoping, that right from the start there'll be an element of trust between us, both ways. You'll have to trust me. And I hope that I'll be able to trust you. Not to change your mind just because you get a better offer.'

Didn't she know that she was the only offer I'd ever had?

'You've agreed to come and live here permanently, and you'll stick to it. Just as I'm going to stick to my side of the bargain.'

'You mean, eternal promises? Like in a marriage, till death us do part?'

She said, 'I've never been married.'

'Nor me.'

We both giggled.

Then I said, 'But at school, in PSHE, we got told about it.'

'Pershee?'

'Personal, Social and Health Education.'

'You got taught about *marriage*?'

'Not really. Just what you have to say. Like how it's for ever and all that.'

Remembering talking with her by the fire made me upset. It was better if I didn't do it. But I couldn't help it.

The chin social worker came to see me again. She asked me how we were all getting along.

I said, 'I dunno. You ask them, not me. They're supposed to be the parents.'

After the chin had gone, I lay on the swirly floor and fiddled with the settings of their video recorder so it'd record a whole load of different programmes than what they'd chosen. When she found out and asked me why, I'd tell her I wanted to broaden her horizons.

Then I went upstairs. Then I came down. Then I went out to their garden. Then I came in again.

Wendy called out to me, 'By the way, dear.'

I thought it was going to be about video recorder resettings.

It wasn't. She obviously hadn't noticed yet.

'When you're not watching the television, would you mind turning it off? It wastes so much electricity. We're not made of money.'

I said, 'Why d'you keep nagging on about money? You get paid enough to have me here, don't you? At the other place I stayed, they didn't keep on about money-money-money all the time. They were glad to have me, just for myself. They didn't get any special allowances for me, like you do.'

I knew she got extra because of the bed thing at night. It counted as a disability. It was supposed to be more work for her, even though I changed the sheets myself. I didn't wet every night but I always stripped off the sheets and put them downstairs where she'd told me to. I didn't want her knowing which nights were wet, which were dry. I wanted her to have to do loads of washing.

'What other place, dear? You mean at your children's home?'

'No, I mean at my other foster parents.'

Wendy tried not to look surprised. She touched her gold earrings, then her watch, as if to check the time. 'I didn't realize you'd been fostered before.'

'Yes,' I said. I lied easily. I'd never spent a night at Evelyn's, though the next bit was true. 'They were going to adopt me.' I called her 'them'. I made myself think of Mr Twitchett as the husband. 'But they were called abroad urgently and they couldn't take me with them.'

'Where did they go?'

'Australia.' Perhaps that *was* where she'd gone? 'Back to their roots.'

'To their what?'

'Roots, roots, roots! Are you deaf? You ought to get a hearing-aid.' I didn't really understand what Evelyn had meant, either. But she'd definitely said it.

She told me, 'Just as my grandparents were pulled towards Tassie by the dream of work and a place of their own, so I was pulled in the other direction. I had this image of Britain. Gentle green fields and orchards. It was so strong. That's what brought me here. I've found it, in a way, with my little cherry tree. But then, just occasionally, I find I miss things from my past. Like the scent of the golden wattle or going to the Sydney fish market on Christmas Eve.'

I said, 'I'm not really from here, either.' I wanted to be like her. Be someone from somewhere else. 'I'm supposed to be Chinese. Twenty-five per cent. I don't feel it.'

'Nor me,' she said. 'I'm supposed to be Scottish. My

grandparents, the ones who sailed to Hobart, they were from Ayrshire. But I've tried eating porridge with salt and shouting, "Hoots mon". It doesn't make me feel close to those particular roots. I think perhaps one's roots are sunk in the place one grew up. That means mine are in a Sydney suburb. Not very glamorous.'

'And mine'd be in Bel'Vue. Worst luck.'

She said, 'You've not finished your growing up yet. There's still time to sink your roots in another place.'

The next time Wendy complained about shortage of money and how I mustn't leave the taps running because it was wasting hot water which didn't heat itself but used up electricity which didn't grow on trees, I told her about the previous foster mother.

'She was incredible. So generous. She'd buy me anything I needed. Even things I didn't need. You should've seen the mountain bike she got me. Derailleurs. Sixteen gears. Fantastic all-terrain grip-tyres. Lithium lamps. Power-lock braking system. Steel chrome frame. She enrolled me at a luxury sports club, too. Olympic-sized pool, jacuzzi, the lot.'

I could see Wendy grinding her teeth as she forced herself not to tell me I was lying. That was a good sight. Daniel would've been proud.

Bob came in from his shed. He'd heard the last bit,

about the bike. 'You sure you aren't having us on?' he said, and winked. Then he said, 'And who's this Daniel you talk about so much?'

'No I don't.'

'OK. But you've mentioned him a few times.'

'He's a sort of relation. A second cousin.'

'Would you like to ask him over? He could stay the night. It might help you feel more settled, to see one of your friends. The social worker's idea. Thinks you ought to mix with more people your own age.'

'Just because I've known someone for a long time doesn't mean I like him.'

'Fair enough. But if you change your mind, let me know.' Bob wasn't as bad as her. At least he was trying to make me happy. He didn't understand. I didn't *want* to be happy. If I got happy, I'd have to stay there.

I did not want this adoption thing. I would not let it happen. I had to get better at being badder. It was the only way of keeping them at bay.

Shop-soiled Goods

She waited till he'd gone out for the shopping so she'd get me alone. Then she started having a go at me.

I was sitting on their swirly carpet in their swirly living-room. I was flicking through a magazine I'd found outside in his shed.

'Would you come through and help with the dishes, pet?' she called. She never used my name.

The magazine suddenly became extra-interesting. There was a travel article with a picture of the Tasmanian devil. I recognized it from the poster I'd nicked and given to Daniel.

She called again, then came through.

At first she didn't say anything. She just held out a tea towel to me and nodded her head towards the plates on the draining-rack in the kitchen. I pretended I didn't understand what she was on about. I went on staring at the picture of the Tasmanian devil and pretending to read the words.

So she came over and put the tea towel in my hand.

'Excuse me,' I said. 'I'm busy reading. An important article about a very rare marsupial from the other side of the world where it's night when it's day here and day down there when it's night here.' I hadn't read all that. I knew from Daniel telling me.

'And I'm busy clearing up,' she said, took the magazine out of my hand and led me to the sink.

'Tea towel,' she said. 'Dishes.' She pointed to them.

'What?' I said.

'The dishes there on the draining-rack, some of which have been utilized by you, some of which your father and I used. They have been washed up. Now all they require is drying and putting away.'

I said, in a low and reasonable voice, 'Why didn't you say so? I can't mind-read.'

She said, 'I thought it would be obvious, even to someone of your intelligence. You've enjoyed the meal, which Bob shopped for and which I have just cleared up. Now it is your turn to offer a modicum of assistance.'

I gave a huge sigh from both lungs, like a warm breeze blowing across from the Tasman Sea, and I began to put her clean dishes away in her cupboards. I stacked them neatly, big plates on big plates, little ones on little.

They all matched. If it hadn't been for her standing there watching, I could have quite enjoyed it. It was like a beautiful puzzle. How to make all her crockery fit tidily so it wouldn't topple over.

But she stopped me. She didn't like the way I was putting them.

'What on earth are you doing? You have to dry them first.'

'They *are* dry,' I said.

She picked one off the top of a tall pile I had made and inspected it. 'No, they're not. This is wet. Please dry them, as requested, before putting them away.'

I said, 'If you say so, Gwendoline. It's your house. But it's unhygienic. Did you know there's more germs on the average tea towel than in a toilet bowl that's just been cleaned with disinfectant?' (Aunty Brenda had told me that.) 'If I wipe anything with this, I'll be smearing germs all over the place. But if that's the way you want it.'

She looked as though she'd explode. 'That tea towel is perfectly clean.'

I said, 'Dishwashers are best. You should get one if you value your long-term health.'

I had the weird feeling I'd been in exactly this place once before, doing this same thing. Daniel had had a special word for it (French, of course). Déjà vu.

Meaning, 'been here before, seen it, done it, got the T-shirt'.

I hadn't really been in that moment before, because you can't travel into the future and back. But I had had a conversation about washing up. Except it had been with Evelyn, not Gwendoline. Weird thing was, at Cherry Tree Cottage I'd got to like being in her kitchen. Washing up was the one and only thing those two women had in common.

She said, 'We don't have money for white-goods luxuries like that.'

I said, 'That's fine, then. Because I don't give a fart how you cope with your dirty dishes because I'm not intending to hang around long enough for it to make any difference to *my* life. So, if you're counting on me as a source of special fostering payments for the rest of your days, don't bother.'

She went to sit in her sitting-room. When I'd finished putting her dishes away, and I took as long as I could because I knew she was listening, she came and said, 'Come and sit down. I think we should have a chat.'

'Yes. Sure. Later. I've just got to go up and do my homework.' I hadn't done any homework since moving to Southdown Avenue. I didn't intend to now. It's a well-known fact (to Sharon, anyhow, who told it to me) that sixty-six per cent of children living in care leave school when they're sixteen without any qualifications. So why should I ruin their statistics by making an effort?

'Extenuating home circumstances' was my excuse to the teachers, day after day. I could say long words even when I couldn't read them.

'It can wait. Please will you sit down.'

I squatted on the carpet with my arms round my folded knees and my back against the swirly wallpaper so I wouldn't topple over.

'Properly. Like a human, not a monkey. On the settee.'

I moved. I sat on the settee, as far from her end as possible.

She said, 'You are not turning out as we expected.'

There was nothing I could say to that, was there?

'As Robert and I expected. We've all been properly assessed, have we not? Us, the parents. You, the child in need.'

I didn't much care for that. I knew I was a mess. There was no need for her to rub it in. But I let it pass.

'Before we were allowed to receive you, we had to go through a complete Home Study. We were not found wanting. We, Robert and I, have been to Panel. We, all three of us, have been Matched and Placed. It's all here in the files.' She pointed to the card file on the coffee table. I knew it as the kind they use at Social Services.

Miss Marshall's office was full of them. Mira with the moustache used them. They all used them. If you wrote things and put them in files, they thought it made sense of life.

She thumped the file angrily with the flat of her hand. 'And it says here that you're an easy-going, likeable boy, responsible, fit in well with other people, enjoy all forms of sport and helping out around the house.' She said it as though she was reading it aloud. She must have learned it off by heart.

I said, 'I didn't write it.'

She said, 'But it was written in consultation with you. They told us.'

I said, 'If you say so. But perhaps it's all lies. Or perhaps I've changed. Or perhaps you have.'

She said, 'This is both our problem. What are we going to do about it?'

I shrugged. She hated my shrugs. 'Personally, I don't have any problem. I'm sorry if you do.'

That was the best thing I could've said. Yippee. She lost her rag completely.

'That's it!' she yelled at me. 'That's it! I have had it up to *here*!' She made a cutting-her-throat movement with her hand, then she stomped out of the room, and upstairs. I heard their bedroom door slam. It made the upstairs landing judder.

I went back to looking at the picture of the Tasmanian devil. It looked fierce, but not very big. I wondered if they roamed about the place so you could see them anytime. I wondered if they attacked humans. I wondered if Evelyn's grandparents had had to worry about Tasmanian devils when they'd been building their flimsy wooden home in the draughty red landscape.

When Bob came in loaded up with supermarket bags, four dangling from each hand, I helped him unpack them and put the stuff away in the fridge and the freezer.

'Thanks, Mak. You're a real help,' he said. 'D'you want to come and help me paint the shed? I could use another pair of hands.'

I said, in a jolly voice, 'Hey that'd be really ace, Bob.' (As though helping a fat forty-year-old with his rotten garden shed would ever be a fun way to pass the time.)

'Yeah, I'd like to. But, Bob, I think you ought to go up and see about your wife first.'

'My *wife*?' He looked blank as though he didn't know what a wife was, let alone that he'd got one.

'Gwendoline,' I said. 'She seemed, well, a bit, you know, upset. Earlier on.'

He looked surprised.

'About me,' I went on, quickly. 'I'm afraid I annoyed

her in some way. If only I knew how. I don't think she likes me much.'

'Of course she does. She's growing very fond of you. She chose you. We both chose you.'

He knew, and I knew, but he didn't know that I knew, that they never chose me. They'd wanted a baby. I was all that was available. Somehow they'd been persuaded to give me a try.

I said, 'Well, whatever. She's really upset.'

He said, 'Is it a mutual thing? Do *you* like her?'

I wasn't expecting that question. What was the answer? I shrugged. For some reason my shrugs didn't annoy him half as much as they annoyed her.

The right answer came into my head. 'Course I do! Gwendoline's a real top person. She's just so kind. I don't know what I'm doing to upset her. Whatever it is, I'll try to make it OK.'

I don't know how the words crawled out of my mouth.

Bob was a simple person. He believed me. He said, 'No, Mak. *You* don't have to make things OK. It's up to us to make it work.'

He went to the stairs. I called after him, 'Nobody said I'd be perfect all the time. You knew all along that you were only getting second-hand goods.'

He paused and rubbed his slobby belly. 'Same for

you. Second-rate parents. You know, you may be only a child but you're a mature boy for your age.'

Then he went on up to her. He was gone ages. I sat and stared out of the window at the house opposite. It looked exactly the same as number 57, but it had an even number. 42. I wondered if it had miserable people living in it.

Later that day, I said sorry to her. I sort of muttered it, with my eyes looking down at the swirly carpet so she'd believe I actually meant it.

She looked at me with tears in her eyes and gave me a light touch on the shoulder. She didn't try to hug me. Thank heaven.

I only did it for the sake of Bob-the-slob. If I said sorry to her, I thought it might make things easier for him. It wasn't his fault she was like she was.

The next day, I said to her, 'By the way, about the dishes and stuff, if you wanted us to save on the washing-up, we could always eat dampers.'

'Dampers?'

'Like the swagmen.'

I wasn't entirely sure what they were either. Evelyn had only said it once.

'In the fire,' I said. 'Bread.' Was it bread? I couldn't remember. Never reveal uncertainty to the enemy, that's what Daniel said. 'Cooked in the fire,' I said firmly.

'Oh, you mean kebabs? Like we cook for barbecues?'

I nodded. I wasn't sure about kebabs. Was it another word for dampers?

'What a peculiar person you are,' she said. 'It's a bit early in the year for a barbecue but, well, you're right. We ought to socialize more.'

At the weekend, they invited some neighbours over. We had a barbecue out in the garden. No question of me helping with any washing-up.

The neighbours had a son. He might have been my age. He might not. We were supposed to get on with each other while the adults chatted, shivered in the cold air, and drank wine.

She was really smooth to me all evening. 'Got everything you need?' she kept saying, silky-sweet. 'Another piece of steak, boys? Oh, my, how they do eat, these growing boys. Amazing. My arms are like elastic. Growing longer every day from the weight of the shopping bags.'

How could she say that? She hardly ever did the supermarket shopping. He did it. Then she complained that he'd bought the wrong stuff and how much easier it was when they'd had a car.

I was amazed how much wine she could drink. Glass after glass. Filled to the brim. At Bel'Vue, nobody drank wine, or beer, except Kevin, who once had a four-pack in his hold-all. I saw it. If you were a care worker, you weren't meant to drink on duty. But obviously, if you were parents, it was different.

The boy and I hadn't much to say to each other. He looked quite clever. The Daniel type. I don't think he wet the bed. So we ate a lot of hard meat, black on the outside, stringy pink inside, then went indoors and watched a video of a comedy show. It must have been recorded aeons ago. You could tell by the clothes they wore. The jokes weren't too hot, either. I don't think he was adopted or fostered. But he didn't seem to get on with his parents. That was a surprise, but I didn't let it show.

He said one thing that was strange.

In the middle of watching the third video of sitcom repeats, he suddenly blurted out, 'I wish we could see into the future.'

I said, 'What for?'

'So we'd know when the horror was going to end.'

I felt sorry for him.

I didn't know that two more bad things were about to happen to me. One seemed as though it would change my life. The other eventually did. I'm glad I couldn't see into the future. Or I'd have seen them coming.

Buena Vista

Wendy and Bob's neighbours had us round to their place for blackened meat inside soft white buns. Same as at 57 except there was a wider choice of videos indoors. The parents there were into martial arts and bird-watching.

The son and I had nothing in common. As before.

Outside on the patio Wendy giggled a lot. I explained to the boy that she wasn't any relation so it needn't embarrass either of us.

As we were coming back to number 57, we heard the telephone ringing inside. Bob fiddled with the front-door key. But he wasn't fast enough. The ringing stopped.

Wendy muttered, 'What a fumbling slowcoach you are!' She was sometimes as sharp with old slobbo as she was with me. 'It might have been urgent.'

I said, 'Have you seen those key-rings with a torch attached? You could get him one for next Christmas.'

Bob said, 'When did we last have an urgent call?'

I said, 'Or you could buy an answerphone.'

She said, 'Too expensive.'

I said, 'No, they're not.'

She said, 'If someone leaves a message, it places the onus on you to call them back. Then the charge goes on your bill, not theirs. It all mounts up. You'll find out soon enough, when you have to pay your own way in life.'

Bob finally managed to get the door open. He had fat fingers as well as a fat belly. He said, 'If it's urgent, they'll try again.'

It must have been. They did.

I was already in bed staring at the masculine wallpaper when the phone rang.

I heard Wendy shouting for me.

'Come down. It's for you!' She sounded irritated.

I went to the top of the stairs.

'Me?'

'It's Georgie. Hurry up. She's waiting.'

'Who?' I came slowly down the stairs. 'I don't know anybody called Georgie.'

'Yes, you do. Don't play the fool.' She thrust the telephone receiver at me.

'Mak, is that you? We've got some simply tremendously thrilling news. It's a real breakthrough.' It was the social worker. 'I'm so glad to have got a chance to speak with you! I've been trying your foster parents' number all evening.'

'We went to a barbecue.'

'Oh wonderful, wonderful. I'm glad you're having lots of fun at last. You do deserve it.'

Fun?

'Now, are you listening carefully? We have found someone, someone very important to you.'

'You found her!' So she hadn't abandoned me. I always hoped she hadn't. I said, 'Thanks. I had an intuition you would.'

'We never thought we would. It's taken a lot of work to track her down. She's in a nursing home and not terribly well. But longing to see you, I'm sure.'

I could hardly hold on to what I was hearing. I felt my face relaxing into a smile for the first time in weeks.

'So I'll come and fetch you tomorrow, first thing. OK?'

You bet it was. I was so excited I couldn't sleep. I tried to guess what had happened.

Perhaps she'd fallen down the stairs? Been tripped up by Mr Twitchett twining himself round her ankles? Perhaps, as she tumbled down the stairs, she'd banged her head on the corner of one of her bookshelves? But the moment she saw my familiar face her lost memory would come flooding back.

The chin's car was even smaller than Mira's.

I said, 'Social Services cutting back?' I meant, as a joke, were they saving money on cars so as to keep paying big foster fees to people like Wendy?

But she didn't hear. Or didn't get it.

I said, 'Not to worry.' I was in a good mood. Now I'd found Evelyn, nearly found, it was OK to let up on the aggro. I listened to her chatter. I nodded. I smiled.

She chattered on. 'I would've popped in more often. But my Team Leader said it was best to leave you to fight your own battles. So it's all coming along OK, then?'

'Dunno. Guess so. More or less.' I smiled and saw myself smiling back from the car's side mirror. I smiled some more. I looked good.

'Wendy says there've been a few ups and downs. I told her not to worry. That's pretty normal for this stage of the game. Honeymoon period over and done. But it seems you're all bonding well enough. So this new development won't rock the boat. In fact, my Team Leader thinks locating your grandmother like this will help the bonding process. Give you an even stronger sense of your own identity.'

I stopped nodding and smiling.

'No. She's not my grandmother. She's my friend. She's

always been my friend.' Because that was how we'd left things between ourselves.

She said, 'Oh yes. Sorry. You never actually lived with her, did you?'

'No. But I was going to.'

'So you never knew her too well?'

'Yes. I mean, no. I don't know.' How well is well?

'Sorry. Hard question. What I mean is, were you fond of each other?'

Yes. Yes. I think I was. I hope she was. I wanted to be, even if I didn't let myself show it.

'Because you may find it quite a shock, how much she's changed. I wouldn't want you to be upset by the change in her.'

'I'll try not to be.'

The nursing home had a sign over the door. 'Buena Vista Home. Your Loved One's Care, Our Priority. Local Authority approved'. It had a locked front door. The care attendant who let us in relocked the door behind us. I thought, Poor Evelyn. To have ended up in a place like this.

She said, 'One or two of our people unfortunately have dementia. They try to go walkies if they can. Not your grandmother, though. She's a sweetie. She's found a little china teapot she wants to give you.'

'She's not actually my grandmother,' I said.

The social worker explained to the care attendant, 'Family friend. That's what he feels most comfortable with.'

The care attendant led us to a large room. Upright armchairs round the walls all faced to the middle. For a moment, I was back in the Day Room at Bel'Vue. It had the same feel. Pretending to be cheerful when it wasn't. There was a telly blaring away on a metal bracket high on a wall, just like at Bel'Vue. But different people. Not children. Here were old women, each sitting or slumping in an armchair covered with stiff plastic. It seemed strange that they had to be locked in. None of them looked as though they could run anywhere. The smell was different from Bel'Vue too.

The care attendant turned down the volume on the telly, then went to one of the armchairs and gently shook the thin arm of the person sitting there.

'Wakey-wakey, May. Here's your lovely grandson come to pay his little visit. Isn't that a nice treat!'

She was small and shrivelled, huddled to one side of her plastic seat so it seemed too wide for her. She was hardly human, more like an old brown monkey. She had thin scrappy hair, almost no teeth. She was Chinese and she definitely wasn't Evelyn.

The care attendant said, 'I told her you were coming

but I'm afraid she's a bit confused today. You'll need to stand closer. She can't see too well.'

I knew she could see me clear enough. A bony chicken's claw reached out from the chair. It grabbed hold of my sweater. The narrow eyes looked up into my face. She began to talk fast, high-pitched. She was telling me something important. I couldn't understand a word.

The care attendant said, 'She *can* speak English if she chooses to. We know she can. The lady who lived next door to her said she could. But now she's here, she won't. A lot of them are like that. The psychologist says it's their return to the security of childhood.'

I could guess what she was saying. She was telling me she hated the place. It was like being thrown into a deep pit. She wanted to get away. It was all her wicked daughter-in-law's fault. Or her son's. Or her husband's. Or perhaps even mine. She was ruining my sweater, pulling on it like that. Wendy would tell me I had no respect even for the clothes on my back.

The attendant rummaged in a cloth bag hanging from the back of the armchair. She found a small object wrapped in yellow newspaper and gave it to me. I took off the paper. Inside was a china teapot. Very small.

She said, 'This is for you. May and I chose it together from among her things. As a keepsake from her to you.'

The floor swung up towards me, and the room

turned round. I had to put out my hand to the back of the chair to steady myself. The scary thing was, I did recognize the teapot. From long ago. I didn't know when, but I'd seen it before. I knew it. It was a greyish colour. It had a Chinese picture on it of some twisty trees and a rock.

The moment I'd taken the little pot from the care attendant, the old monkey's claw let go of my sweater and grabbed up for it.

'Now, May. Remember how we talked about this?' said the attendant gently. 'About giving something to the boy? As a memento?'

I was startled by her grabbing for it. I held on tight so as not to let the teapot slip out of my hand. But her claw was stronger than my hand. She got her bony fingers round the handle and tugged. Then the teapot dropped to the floor with a tinkle.

'Oh no!' said the attendant. She looked really upset. 'What a shame. I know she intended you to have it.'

I knew she hadn't.

She'd deliberately lost her grip on the teapot. Now she lost her grip on everything else. She turned her face away from us all. She stared at the shiny plastic side of her chair.

Anyway, what would I want with a teapot? I don't drink tea. Or coffee.

The care attendant said, 'I'm really sorry about this. She's not at her best today.'

The social worker said, 'These family reunions can be rather overwhelming, can't they?'

I was glad to leave behind the smell of wee and packet soup. I sat in the car without speaking.

'Well?' said the social worker as she started up the engine.

I didn't reply. I thought, She wasn't Evelyn. I was expecting Evelyn.

After several miles, the social worker couldn't bear the silence. 'Well?' she said. 'You're very pensive. Penny for your thoughts.'

'Haven't got any.'

Of course I had. But it was just one thought, and too straightforward for her.

She said, 'So what d'you think? How does it feel to meet up with your own flesh and blood after so long? Or was it all a bit much to take in on one visit?'

I said, 'I was expecting Evelyn.'

She glanced at me quickly. 'May. Her name is May. She's your grandmother.'

I said, 'You shouldn't do that, take your eyes off the road. You might crash into something. You'd lose your licence.'

She said, 'She's your natural father's mother. I did explain.'

'Yes. I know. I remembered her.'

'Good. She responded to you, didn't she? And that little teapot, it's so quaint. It looks old. Perhaps she had it in her dowry. I've got all the pieces here. I'm sure Bob could fix it with a dab of that special glue for china.'

I said, 'It's all right. It's only a thing that's broken. It's not like a person.'

'You're very strong, Mak. I admire you. D'you know, I almost believe she did it on purpose, letting it go like that?'

I said, 'No, it was me. I let it go.'

No. It was she who'd made that grab for it. It was she who'd made it fall. She didn't want me to have it. And I'd understood. She didn't want me. And that was fine because I didn't want her. So we were quits.

I said, 'She's Chinese.'

She said, 'Is that why you find it hard to accept her as your kin?'

'I didn't say that. I just don't want her for my grandmother.'

'Mak, love, you know you'll have to face up to your ethnic identity some day soon. You can't deny it forever.'

I said, 'I need to see Evelyn. I have a right to.' I

thought, And if you don't know who Evelyn is, look her up in your files.

'Evelyn Cairns?'

'Yes.'

That kept her quiet for so long that at last I had to say, 'Well?'

'Well what?'

'Will you tell me how I can find her?'

I thought, Instead of dredging up half-dead grandmothers, why don't you look for the one that matters? That's who I want to live with. That's who I'm *going* to live with.

The chin didn't reply at once. She waited till we'd reached a lay-by, then pulled over and stopped the car.

She spoke directly to the steering wheel. 'I cannot believe I'm hearing right. Tell me it's wrong. This is absolutely dreadful. We'll have to have a reappraisal of our information conveyancing.'

At first, I thought we must have a puncture.

She went on and on. Then I realized it was me she was talking to, not the car.

'I cannot believe you've been left in the dark so long. Evelyn Cairns is completely out of the picture. You mean, you *really* didn't know, you're not just making it up?'

'Making what up?'

'She died months ago.'

In for a Penny, in for a Pound

I trudged towards the stairs. My legs were like rotten wood. I thought they'd crumble before I reached my masculine room. Downstairs in the hallway, the chin was telling them what'd happened. Bob was listening with his mouth slightly open. Wendy was nodding her head.

'He's overwhelmed. It's inevitable. We had a demanding outing. These blood links are so important to maintain. Though whether blood's really thicker than water is anyone's guess. Still, he's a sturdy little lad. You're lucky to have picked him.'

'Heavy seas, difficult times,' Bob said in a gloomy voice.

'Oh the poor wee lamb,' Wendy said. She was only trying it for effect.

'Safe port ahead,' Bob said, which I doubted.

The social worker went on with her debriefing. 'We

may even have to consider bereavement counselling.'

Wendy nodded some more.

'Even when children are strong, they need communication and support. But we'll try to avoid psychiatric intervention if we can. My hunch is, he'll be right as rain after a good night.'

Wendy nodded and nodded like an electronic nodding Santa on a Christmas tree.

'Sleep's the best medicine,' said the chin. 'Feel free to ring the office anytime. I'm away on in-service training all next week, but my colleagues will speak to you. Or, if it's out of hours, try the Duty Officer.'

I heard her leave. I thought, Nobody who knew would ever ring the Duty Officer. They'd get more help calling the RSPCA.

When I reached my room, my woodwormed legs crumpled. I fell face down on the masculine maroon and chocolate-brown duvet stripes. I heard the plastic undersheet crackle. For a while, I snivelled. Sobbing for that mottled old monkey who hadn't got anybody except a paid care attendant to take any notice of her.

But then I remembered things. I thought, If she'd wanted someone, she should've taken *me*, way back on that night when Maureen ran round with me. Bundled in a grubby yellow blanket. To the housing block. Into the lift which was jammed. Out of the lift. Up the concrete stairs. To the flat on the sixth floor. Maureen hammered on the door. She tried to make the old woman take me. If the old monkey had reached out her arms to me then, she'd still have me now. But she didn't. She closed the door in Maureen's face. End of story.

In the night, Evelyn came to find me. I heard creaking along the landing. I opened my door. She was in her big patchwork skirt, with bare feet, brown like hen's feet. She was smiling. She beckoned. I followed her downstairs. The front door stood wide open. Beyond was no longer Southdown Avenue but a bright open place with red dusty ground and a mob of grandparents putting up their flimsy wooden huts while the wind moaned in the telegraph wires.

Then it started again. Evelyn came creaking along the landing. I sat up in bed. I got up. I followed her as before. I saw her trip at the top of the stairs and fall. I saw it again, only the next time she didn't trip. Wendy scuttled out from under the wainscotting and pushed her from behind. She toppled and slowly fell. Her long legs were struggling in space like an emu trying to fly.

In the daytime I didn't think about her at all. It was as though she'd never existed. But at night, every night, she came back and back and back and fell down the

130

stairs so many times she must have been bruised from head to foot.

Some nights she flung herself down the stairs. Some nights I nudged her. Most nights it was Wendy.

One night, I managed to wake myself just as Evelyn started her slow float down the stairs. Once I'd started screaming for her to watch out, I couldn't stop.

The lights went on. They came staggering out of their room.

'What in heck's going on now?' she said.

They wore matching pyjamas, shiny like their jogging suits. Bob's hair wasn't tied back in its ponytail. It was hanging slack on his shoulders.

I hadn't seen them in their nightclothes before. I hadn't seen any adults in their nightclothes, not since the night when Maureen was hammering on the door of the old monkey's flat and a neighbour came out in her nightgown and phoned for the police.

The noise went on coming out of my mouth, out of my ears. They asked me what the matter was. I couldn't tell them. I couldn't stop myself screaming.

'Give him a slap!' she said. 'A quick, hard slap. You've got to shock him out of it.'

Bob wouldn't do it, so she did. I didn't even feel it. But I knew it was wrong. *I* was the one who went round hitting people in the face, not her.

Bob peered close into my slapped face. 'What–is–it–you–want–us–to–do?' he begged. 'Tell–us. Tell–us–what–it–is–and–we'll–help–you.'

'Evelyn!' I screamed. 'I want Evelyn!'

'Tell him he can't. We've got to stop this racket!' said Wendy. 'What'll the neighbours think? They'll start reporting us for child battering.'

Bob said, 'Mak, your friend's gone away.'

Wendy said, 'Tell him the truth. They found something nasty. It was terminal.'

I didn't know what that meant. It made no difference.

'It means cancer, you ignorant boy. The big C. In an aggressive form.'

They used to call me aggressive. That was at school. I hadn't hit anyone for a while.

I'd been kept from Evelyn and it had to be someone's fault.

Wendy started yelling at me to stop screaming. I started yelling back at Wendy, that it was her fault. And it was. She'd killed Evelyn on purpose so she could have me herself.

'Of course that's not true! How could it be! We didn't even know the poor old dear.'

'Old!' I screamed. 'Who said she was old? She wasn't old. She was never old. She was young at heart.' It was Mira who'd told me that Evelyn was young at heart.

Wendy wanted to try another of the slaps.

Bob said, 'No. They don't work.'

So they tried ice cubes down my back and wet flannels on my head. It didn't help.

So much hullabaloo. People at Bel'Vue often had screaming fits. What type of adults were these if they couldn't cope with one howl? Lucky they never got a baby placed with them. Babies scream non-stop. Maureen had told me. 'Drives you crazy in the end,' she'd said.

'For goodness' sake, Bob! We've got to do something. He's completely hysterical.'

It was true. The screaming had taken over so I could hardly breathe. The snot was building up inside my head. The screams were blocking my throat. I would die of suffocation.

Bob went and rang the numbers he'd been given. Wendy stood on the landing, drumming her fingernails on the banister rail and looking at her watch.

He came back. 'They're all switched over to their answerphones.'

So they called up Bel'Vue. They got Aunty Brenda. They must've hauled her out of bed. They dragged me down to the telephone.

'It's your friend on the other end,' said Bob. 'Your aunty.'

They held the phone to my ear. They got her to talk to me. I screamed back into the mouthpiece. 'She's died! Why did she die? What made her die? I want her. You had no right. Nobody had any right.'

Poor Aunty Brenda. She didn't know what was going on any more than I did. 'Why, every dog must have its day,' she said, which even in my state I knew wasn't helpful. It made me howl some more. I was a wild dog. I was not having my day.

I raged back up the stairs on all fours, no longer a dog, but a Tasmanian devil whose teeth are so sharp they can slice through bone.

In the end they managed to get someone because I could hear them taking turns on the phone explaining how to find the way to Southdown Avenue.

Bob came up. 'She's coming round to see you,' he said. 'The manager woman. Try and hold on, old pal, till she gets here. Harbour lights ahead.'

Miss Marshall? Coming here? At first, I didn't believe him. That wasn't the sort of thing she did – get involved.

Aunty Brenda must have given them the number even though she's not meant to. When a person's off-duty, they're off, and that's it. Like off the face of the earth. Not existing any more. You don't ring them up about *anything*.

And she did turn up. I recognized the sound of her car.

I heard the door-chimes. Heard them go to the door. Heard them speak to her. Heard her coming up the stairs. Alone. Without them. I kept my eyes shut, but even in the darkness, behind my puffy eyelids, I knew it was her. She sat on the bed. She never got too close. She didn't like to be messed up. She knew that children messed you up. I had snot, the wet and the dry, all over my face, and dribble coming from my mouth. I was even wetter than if I'd peed myself.

She handed me a clean paper tissue. She had a whole packet with her.

'Wipe your face now, Mak.' She spoke firmly but not angrily. 'Blow your nose. And then I'm going to help you out of here so we can sort this thing out.'

She pulled a sweater on over my pyjamas and then led me downstairs. I followed like a dumb-wit dog. I didn't look at them. They were cowering in their hall. They knew they'd failed. They were afraid to look at me. The boy they'd been given, being taken away. Serve them right.

She helped me into her car. She clipped up the seat belt for me. She wasn't in her stiff blue suit. She was wearing jeans and a rugby sweatshirt, almost like a normal person. But nothing was normal. It was the

135

middle of the night. We were driving through empty streets and I was wearing pyjamas.

She took me to her home. Her own personal home. For so many years I'd never set foot inside a home. Now, in the short space of months, I'd been inside three.

She lived with a woman who called her 'Jean'. I never even thought of Miss Marshall having a personal name.

'Hi, Jean,' said the other woman. 'So you found it all right. You weren't gone long.'

'It was fine,' said Miss Marshall. 'No traffic. Angie, this is Mak. Mak, this is Angie.'

'Hi there,' the woman said to me. 'We don't have a spare room. But I've made up a bed for you on the couch in Jean's study. OK?'

I tried to say something, but it didn't come out. I nodded.

Miss Marshall brought me a toothbrush, new, still in its wrapper. 'I usually keep a spare for my nieces,' she said. 'Sorry it's got a Mickey Mouse handle. I remember you don't much care for childish things.'

She showed me where their downstairs toilet was, told me which lights would stay on all night and said we would talk in the morning. She said, 'Goodnight. Hope you can get some sleep. You look as though you need it.'

I managed to mumble back, 'G'night, Miss Marshall'.

136

I surprised myself. An hour ago I'd been boiling myself into a such a turmoil that I couldn't even breathe, let alone speak.

Weird how she didn't seem half as bad as she used to be at Bel'Vue.

She went halfway out of the room, then came back.

'Listen, Mak, this is completely off-limits. To bring you back here. You know that, don't you? Course you do. But Angie's a good sport. She says it's fine by her. I ought to be doing my nut getting hold of the Duty Officer to find Emergency Accommodation for you.'

'I wouldn't mind,' I muttered. 'Going back to Bel'Vue for the night.' Now I was snug under a sheet and a blanket and a checked rug, it was easy enough to say. If it'd make it easier for her. I wouldn't want her to get into trouble.

'It wouldn't be Bel'Vue. It's full. It'd probably have to be out of county. Miles away. Some unknown would have to drive you there. But it doesn't seem the right thing for you. You'd lose all you've been gaining. Well, goodnight again.'

I went to sleep puzzled. What did she think I'd gained?

In the morning over breakfast they were both, matter-of-fact, as though it was no big deal having me there eating toast and drinking grapefruit juice. I might always have been there. None of the fuss, like at Wendy's, over whether I was a messy eater or put too much marmalade on the spoon.

Miss Marshall was in her off-duty clothes. The other one, Angie, was in a suit. She rushed off to work with a piece of toast in her hand. She was a teacher. I'd never seen a teacher who wasn't in a school.

'Angie's deputy head of a big primary,' Miss Marshall said. 'Loves it. But somehow always manages to leave home late. She'll be stuck in the rush hour. But now, what about you? Are you intending to go to school today?'

'Suppose so.'

'You can't go like that, can you? I'm off to my gym at ten. I'll drop you off at home on the way.'

I said, 'Not back to them!'

'Where else? A park bench suit you?'

'Couldn't I stay here and, you know, live with you?'

I began to remember things about her, from long ago. At Bel'Vue she'd taught me stuff. It wasn't her job. But she'd done it anyway. How to wipe my bum, to wash my hands, to pour out the milk and lift the mug to my mouth to drink.

'And you can learn to read, too,' she'd said one time. 'Quite soon.'

So what'd gone wrong? If she'd been there to help, what had stopped me?

I said, 'I wouldn't be any trouble. I'd go to school every day and help wash up and all sorts of stuff.'

She smiled. But it was a No-smile.

'Sorry, Mak. It wouldn't work. Why do you think I haven't got any children of my own? Because I never wanted any. Because I always knew I wouldn't be any good at it. Angie never wanted children, either. Luckily, we found each other.'

I said, 'You're OK with little kids. Like with Maisie. You were great with her, even when nobody else was.'

'People like me and Angie, we can be good managing children in a professional way, from a distance, for a short time. That's not the same thing as parenting.'

She'd never talked to me like this before, like I was an adult. She'd never talked to me. Stop.

'A person needs *quite* other skills to be a good parent, even a half-good one. Nobody's yet worked out what those precise skills are. If only we did, it might be easier to identify good parents. Or maybe what constitutes good parenting skills is different for every family combination.'

I wondered if Evelyn had those skills. It felt as though she did. Now I'd never know. I felt a weep coming on again.

'I liked being with Evelyn,' I cried.

'Of *course* you did. Who wouldn't? She sounds like she was a fine woman. But now you've got to give it a go with Robert and Gwendoline.'

'I'll think about it,' I sniffed.

'Do more than think about it. Really try.'

'I have tried.'

'Not very hard, I'll bet.'

'You don't know what they're like,' I said, with a whine sneaking in where the sob had been. '*You* wouldn't want them for parents.'

'I'm serious, Mak. Given your age, this placement is likely to be your last chance. It's probably their last chance too. *You're* not the person *they* wanted. *They're* not the people *you* wanted. Somehow, all of you have got to meet halfway and try to make it work. For all of your sakes.'

'I want to be back with Evelyn.'

'We all want to go back to the best bits, leaving out the bad. But nobody can go back in time. It's a terrible tragedy that she died. But the world is full of tragedies and, sadly, some of them a good deal graver than yours.'

I liked her using the word, 'tragedy'. There was a medium-sized tragedy going on and I was a part of it. I said, 'Sometimes I think it'd have been best if I'd died, too.'

'What nonsense! You've got your whole life ahead of you. Though I suppose you might feel better if you'd never met her and been spared all this extra unhappiness.'

No, I thought. That would've been much worse. I said, 'I had some intuitions that maybe weren't real. But I'm sure it was my destiny to meet Evelyn Cairns.'

Miss Marshall smiled. 'Well done. That's the spirit.'

On the drive back to 57 Southdown Avenue, she stopped at a petrol filling station.

'Take her some flowers,' she said. 'They often work wonders with difficult people.'

'Flowers?'

'As a gesture of goodwill.'

Outside the cashier's booth stood bags of barbecue charcoal and a black rubber bucketful of flowers.

'Got any money on you? No, of course you haven't. How could you. Here. Have this.' Miss Marshall handed me a couple of quid. 'Out you hop.'

I picked out a bunch from the bucket. They were all much the same, brightly-coloured and windswept. I paid for them and gave Miss Marshall back the change.

'Good lad,' she said. 'Offer them to her as soon as you get in. You don't have to say anything. See if they do the trick.'

Making a Mark

Only Bob was home. So I had to give them to him. He looked mystified. He tugged at his ponytail and rubbed his belly.

'Never been given a bouquet by a bloke before,' he said. But he took them from me. I think he was pleased.

I got into my uniform. I buzzed off to school. When I got home, I said I'd do tea. I cooked pasta. I boiled it up. It went grey and soggy. I wasn't expecting that to happen.

I said, 'Wow. What a mess. Sorry. I thought you had to cook it like spuds.'

Wendy sighed.

I covered it with some ready-serve sauce, tomatoes and stuff, out of a jar.

He ate it. I ate it. He said it was the best he'd ever had. *She* pushed it round her plate like Sharon used to. She didn't eat it.

'You're supposed to heat up the sauce,' she said. 'In a pan, not pour it on cold.'

She never said a word about the bunch of flowers in the vase, though Bob pointed them out to her.

She was probably right. They weren't good value. They shrivelled up the next day. It was probably from the petrol fumes that'd been wafting round on the forecourt.

I cleared up the meal. I washed up, including the sticky pasta pan. I wiped the cooker.

Every day, in every way, I was changing.

Other people were trying their best for me, too, specially about Evelyn. Miss Marshall drove me to the cemetery outside town to see where Evelyn was buried. We stood together and looked at the plot. There was nothing to say it was hers.

I said, 'I suppose there's been no one to do anything about it. She didn't have relations.'

Miss Marshall said, 'It seems some of her colleagues have made a collection and are going to arrange for a headstone.'

'Her *whats*?'

'The people she worked with. She was at the FE college.'

'Oh,' I said. 'Another teacher.'

Miss Marshall said, 'Do you have a picture of her?'

'No.'

'Would you like one, because the college probably has some. I could ask.'

'No. It's all right. I'll make do with the pictures in my head.'

'Yes. You're probably right. They're more reliable.'

I had another new social worker. She thought my case was very interesting. She got me on the waiting list for bereavement counselling. She said it would be a special time, when I could talk about my feelings and share my grief. So I grinned and said that if my turn came up I'd be willing to give it a try if she thought it'd be good for me.

'Well,' she said, 'the service is intended for children when a close family member has passed away. Particularly in violent circumstances.'

'What, like a car crash or falling downstairs?'

'Yes, or when one parent murders the other.' She sounded interested in the possibilities. 'That can be a very difficult situation for a child to come to terms with. So it's unusual to be seeking counselling when the deceased was someone you scarcely knew.'

I listened. I didn't protest that Evelyn was the closest family member I'd ever had.

I quickly got to the top of the waiting list. I said to the

new social worker, 'Perhaps not so many parents have been killing each other this year?' I meant it as a joke. She didn't get it.

The sessions were just the same as any other counselling I'd ever had.

'Do you want to talk about your feelings?' the counsellor asked.

'No,' I said, because I didn't know what my feelings were. I'd never known someone who'd died before.

'You may feel angry with your friend,' the counsellor suggested. 'That's quite an OK way to feel.'

'No,' I said. 'Why should I? It wasn't her fault. Unless she'd killed herself on purpose. But she didn't.'

When I was really angry, like at school most days, I felt I had to hit someone before I could feel better. But it wasn't like that thinking about Evelyn.

The counsellor said, 'Holding on to your important memories while letting go and moving towards a new future is a huge challenge.'

I said, 'Yes. It must be.'

I thought, How can you hold on and let go at the same time?

She said, 'Do you understand what I mean?'

I said, 'No, not really, because if a person was halfway up a rope-ladder and was told to hold on by one teacher and to let go by another, both at once, the person would crash to the ground and they'd probably break their neck, at least both their arms, wouldn't they?'

The counsellor agreed that they probably would.

The next time I saw her, she asked if I'd feel more comfortable making a Memory Box instead of talking.

I said, 'No, thank you,' very politely.

Although I didn't like talking to the counsellor about Evelyn, sometimes after the session I'd talk to Bob. Mostly, he didn't have any good ideas about Memory Boxes. He just listened.

But one Saturday he took me to find Cherry Tree Cottage. 'Just for a quick peek,' he said.

It looked sad. There was a builder's van outside and a bath lying on its side where the cherry tree used to be.

'Heave-ho. Looks like renovation time,' said Bob. 'Area must be going up. Should be worth a bob or two.'

I thought that was funny, Bob saying, 'a bob or two'.

He said, 'An old man I knew used to say it. I used to weed his garden. A bob meant a shilling. Five pence.'

I said, 'I'm sure a house must be worth more than two bob. That's only ten pence.'

Bob scratched his knee. 'I reckon so, too.'

We watched the builders wheeling barrowloads of rubble out of Evelyn's front door, which was strange because, although her house had been full of plenty of junk and jumble, there hadn't been any rubble.

I said, 'What would've happened to all her stuff?'

'What stuff?'

'Inside. She had loads of special things.'

There was her souvenir collection of picture drying-up cloths, ironed and folded in the kitchen drawer. And the teaspoons, polished to make them happy. Jugs, books, bits of coloured sea glass, cricket stumps. Lace mats and a forty-million-year-old fossil.

Bob said, 'I dunno. I dare say a house-clearance firm was called in.'

I said, 'Someone who hadn't got a home could've lived in that house.'

Bob said, 'Someone probably will, soon enough. When they've finished their renovations.'

'I mean, as it was. It had everything you'd need. You could've moved straight in.'

'People don't usually want other people's old bits and pieces. They usually want their own.'

Like children, I thought. But I didn't say it because I was trying to be an easy child. Instead, I said, 'She had a cat. I wonder if it's all right?'

'Very independent creatures, cats. Go their own way. Might be living rough. More likely, it found itself a new place. I had a cat once. Stayed a year, decided it didn't like me, moved off to some other folks down the road.'

We walked back to 57 Southdown Avenue. We didn't talk about Evelyn's house any more. I was putting it behind me, or so I thought.

We still didn't have anything in common, him and me, but we weren't getting on too badly. She was the one who went on being annoying. I made an effort. She stayed the same.

One day, without a warning, she asked, 'Have you thought about your name?'

What was she on about now? I didn't say anything in case it was wrong. I went on shovelling up Coco Pops into my mouth.

She said it again, louder, in a wheedling voice. 'Have you thought about a change of name, when we adopt you?'

'If,' I spluttered through the Coco Pops. She leaped for the kitchen-paper towels to blot up the splutter. '*If* you adopt me.' The decision was still mine.

'Don't worry. There'll be no more delays. The paperwork's nearly done. No more ifs in your life. Any day now we should receive the call to go to court. And when it occurs, when it goes through, that's the obvious time for the name-change, if we are considering it. Your surname will anyway be changing to ours, won't it?'

Would it? I hadn't thought about that yet. There were so many other things to think about. 'Steady on. You're rushing me,' I said. I remembered when my key worker back at Bel'Vue had been doing the Preparation For Family Life with me, there'd been so much information I hadn't taken much in. She'd said, 'There'll be plenty of time, Mak. No one's expecting you to swallow it all at once.'

Another thing she'd said, I thought she'd said, 'You don't *have* to change your surname. Every adoptee feels differently. Some can't wait to get rid of a previous name and start a new life. Others may want to start something new, but to hold on to what they were before. Neither way is right. Or wrong. It's specially relevant to children who're going to be steps.'

'Steps?' I'd said.

'Stepchildren. When the stepfather or stepmother adopts them, which may well be to their advantage, the child might choose to retain their previous surname. It's quite normal. So, whatever you decide, it'll be your choice.'

Wendy said, 'So I thought, we thought, that this would be the time to change your first name.'

'How d'you mean, change it?'

'Bob thinks so, too.'

'Why would I want to do that?'

'Yours isn't a very usual name, is it?' It certainly wasn't usual to her. She never used it. 'You probably haven't noticed while you've been young. But as you're growing up you might find it quite a handicap.'

'Handicap's rude. You shouldn't say that. You're meant to say "disability".'

One of the girls back at Bel'Vue had a disability. It meant she sometimes couldn't understand things and she ate too many sweets. Aunty Brenda told her it wasn't healthy for people with Down's syndrome to put on extra weight because of their hearts. I knew I hadn't got Down's syndrome, even though Daniel sometimes said I must have, because of my slanting eyes.

I said to Wendy, 'It's not in my Life Book that I'm disabled.'

Wendy got flustered. She fiddled with her earrings. 'I'm so sorry, pet. I don't mean to insult you. Of course you're not dumb. Not at all. Quite the opposite. You're a bright boy, in your own way. You just haven't had the chances. That's what your social workers all say. And that's why I thought, we thought, Bob and I thought, you should have the best chance in the world. And it would really assist you in your future, we felt, if you had a name that was more common, more usual. More like Mike, or Mick. Nearly the same as Mak, just a vowel or two. What about Timothy? That's a nice name. If we'd had a child of our own, we were planning on calling him Timothy.'

I stared at her. I felt myself opening and closing my mouth like a goldfish. Taking in air. Letting it out. In a tiny fish voice I heard myself saying, 'I'm Mak. I'm me.'

'It was just an idea.'

'If you change my name—' I began. But I didn't know how to finish. I didn't know what would happen, if anything. I just felt that she wanted to change all of me, starting with my name and then the rest of me, to turn me into the boy-person she'd always dreamed of. Only that sort of boy didn't exist. Not inside me, anyhow.

I left my Coco Pops bobbing in their brown milk. I went up to my room. Still not properly my room. Never my room. Always Wendy's second-best spare room that she'd got ready for her dream-child called Mick or Mike, or Timothy, but who was certainly not me.

I put my school-bag on the bed. I opened it up. I took out my pen case. I took out a felt-tip pen. It was brown. A masculine colour. On the wall beside the bed I wrote 'Mak'.

It was where I would see it when I lay down. I'd see it before I went to sleep. I'd see it again when I woke up in the morning. I'd be able to lie with my head on the pillow and see it without turning my body, just moving my eyes. It would remind me who I was.

I'd lost Evelyn. I didn't want to lose myself as well.

It felt good writing with indelible brown ink on her new wallpaper. The ink sank in so you couldn't rub it off.

I took another pen, green this time, and wrote a green 'Mak', larger than the first.

I took out all the colours, orange, red, pale blue, dark blue, black, grey, pink, yellow, mauve. I wrote 'Mak' in each colour. I remembered Daniel's black line on the carpet which he called his Equator. This was better. This was a rainbow.

Next, I wrote 'I am Mak', then 'Mak is me'. Then I wrote more 'Maks'. *Mak Mak   Mak Mak Mak   Mak Mak Mak Mak   Mak Mak Mak Mak Mak Mak*

Mak Mak Mak Mak   Mak Mak Mak

Mak Mak   Mak Mak Mak   Mak Mak Mak Mak

Mak Mak   Mak   Mak Mak Mak Mak Mak Mak
over the entire wall.

A new wallpaper pattern.

This way, that way, up down and over the Irish Sea. I wrote it round the light switch, and the edge of the mirror and behind the masculine striped curtains and the curtain tiebacks.

It looked good.

I pushed the wardrobe to one side. On the wall behind it I wrote, 'Mick, Mack, I am not Nick Nack Paddywhack. I am not Sebastian, Paul, Malcolm, John,

Kalam, Mark, Christopher, Peter, Zak, Kashif, Graham, Amrin, Horace, Sri, Sam.' I wrote the name of every boy in my class that I was not. When I ran out of boys' names, I went back to Maks, till every space was filled and my hand was aching from the effort.

I stood back to admire my work. It felt good. It was good. It was flipping brilliant. The walls were chortling. The room was mine.

That was the moment I decided to take Miss Marshall's advice. I'd stay with them at 57. At least for as long as a cat.

I glanced up. I noticed the ceiling. White. Untouched. Urgently in need of the Mak treatment.

'Hey, ceiling! You'll have to wait!' I called out. 'Till another day. All good things come to them that wait!'

If I was staying, I had all the time in the world to sort out the place to my own satisfaction.

Or so I thought.

But next day came the news from the solicitors. Not about adoption, but about my Evelyn.

Master Moneybags

I could tell the second I stepped through the kitchen door that something was up. She'd told me I was to come in from school by the back. She didn't like her carpet in the front hall getting used up.

And what's a carpet for if it's not for walking on with mucky trainers, for flip's sake? When she wasn't around, I walked on it anyway, back and forth, just to make sure it was being used for its proper purpose.

She wasn't in her kitchen waiting to pounce, to ask if I'd had a nice day, pet, and to remove my shoes, pet, before I come a step further indoors, all right, pet?

Relief. Then anxiety. What would make her abandon her 4.35 lookout position?

I listened.

She was in her swirly front room. So was Bob. So was the latest social worker, even though it wasn't her day for checking up on me. And so was another person, a man in a black suit. I'd never seen him before. Was he director of Social Services? Had Wendy phoned them up? Had I gone too far with the wallpaper stunt? Had she had enough of me just when I'd decided I might as well stay?

I dithered. I started to creep silently towards the stairs so I could lie low.

Wendy called out, 'Is that you, Mak?' At least she used my name.

'Yes.' Who else did she think it would be? Bob's secret lover?

Slob-a-Bob rubbed his belly nervously and patted the chair next to him. I went on standing in the doorway of the sitting-room.

'Yes?'

'We've some important information here, Mak,' said the social worker. 'All about you.' She was smiling. 'It turns out you're a lucky young fellow. This is Mr Sloane, the executor.'

The man in the suit stood up, came over and shook my hand, which seemed an odd thing for an executor to do.

'Who's got to be executed?'

He thought that was so funny he went on pumping my hand up and down.

'Executor,' he said. 'Not executioner.'

I'd got the words wrong. One of my teachers once said, 'If you read more, you know more.' But I hadn't, so I didn't.

'No persons will be executed,' the man in the suit went on. 'But a bequest will be. Let me explain in simple terms. I was appointed by the testator to carry out the provisions of the will in which Miss E. Cairns named you, and one other party, as the sole two beneficiaries of her estate.'

Some explanation. What did all that mean?

Wendy gasped.

The social worker said, 'You've been left quite a lot of money, Mak.'

I said, 'I don't see how. She wasn't rich. She got her clothes from charity shops and she collected stones and stuff. Broken glass and old tea towels.'

The executor said, 'She owned a house. That is what is relevant to you.'

I said (because that's what Bob had said), 'Worth a bob or two.'

The executor laughed again. 'So it would seem. Even after payment of the IHT, there remains a tidy sum for each of the beneficiaries.'

I said, 'Who's the other person?' I hoped it might be Mr Twitchett.

'The other beneficiary is not a single individual, but

a small village in South America. I believe it is where Miss Cairns worked as a volunteer some years ago.'

'Well, I never. An inheritor of wealth in our midst! Time to push out the boat!' said Bob and he gave me one of his special winks, which I pretended not to notice.

Wendy, trying not to look eager, said to the social worker, 'And how long have you known?'

'A wee while. It had to go through probate. And our Team Leader didn't want the information to influence your own decision about Mak. I knew it wouldn't. When you want a child, you want that child along with all his baggage, don't you, the good and the bad?'

Wendy wouldn't want me for my money? You bet she would.

The executor said, 'Now young man, is there anything you'd like to ask?'

'Yes. What's the IHT?'

'Aha! You're a bright lad, I can see. Asking all the right questions,' said the executor and he explained about the laws of inheritance taxation. It seemed that, even after you're dead, you still have to pay tax to the government.

I said, 'I geddit. So there's enough money to pay pensions to the old folk and foster fees to people who look after kids like me?'

The executor smiled. 'Hm. That's about the sum of it.'

Wendy glared as though she hated me. Or perhaps it was Evelyn she hated, because Evelyn was giving me something that Wendy couldn't.

The social worker said, 'I'm sure a rise in pocket money will be in order in the near future, wouldn't you say, Wendy?'

After they'd gone, Wendy sent Bob out to the offy. They opened a bottle of wine and clinked glasses and said, 'Cheers, Mak!' because I'd come into money.

'Something fishy here,' I said and went upstairs.

I was trembling all over, like it was a freezing cold day. I'd been pretending to be cheerful. But inside I was all chewed up. I lay on my bed and thought about the letter I wanted to write to her. It was better than doing it for real, because I didn't have to go and ask Wendy for an envelope or a stamp, and I didn't have to spell the words, because when you write inside your head to somebody who's dead the spelling comes right by itself.

Dear Evelyn, I don't want your legacy. It's no flipping use to me. Billions and trillions and squillions of pounds are no good I need happiness and feeling I am someone and I belong somewhere and not being sad all the time And not wishing I wasn't me That's what I need So why give me a legacy? Why didn't you hang around a bit longer? That would have been a whole heap more use to me

> You're a stupid woman for being dead I wish you hadn't
> made things so difficult for me by making me get to like
> you. That doesn't mean I wish I'd never met you.

I didn't dream about her any more. I tried to. Even bad
dreams would've been better than an empty blank.

After a few days I got used to the shock of being
someone who had nearly ninety thousand pounds in
the bank. Wendy didn't let me forget it, either. She
thought about it a lot. And she had loads of ideas how
I should spend it.

'You could get yourself built a lovely spacious
extension room, like a sun lounge, on the end of the
kitchen where the old lean-to is.'

'What would I want that for?'

'So you'd have more space. A growing boy needs
space. It's not good to spend so much time up in your
bedroom. It only makes you do silly things.'

'I like my bedroom,' I said. Specially now I'd got rid
of the curtains and the lampshade and the wardrobe
and the bed and just slept on the mattress on the floor.

'Or you could have a swimming pool, in the garden.
Tiled blue, with a heater and all. You said you were
good at swimming. You could take a dip any time you
fancied. That boy from down the road, he could come
over for a swim. And his parents.'

Yeah, I thought, or I could buy myself my very own house, far away from you.

She didn't give up.

'What about a car of your own?'

Was she off her head? I said, very reasonably, 'You have to be seventeen before you're allowed to drive. And you have to pass a written test about the Highway Code.'

She said, 'Yes, of course. We'd drive it for you, but it'd still be your car. Wherever you wanted to go, we'd take you. Wouldn't we, Bob?'

Bob nodded. 'Good idea. Rolls-Royce suit? I'll bet he'd prefer a Harley Davidson. Or what about a race-horse? Or a sailing yacht.'

'Bob!' she said sharply. 'I'm serious.'

I could guess how long Wendy, my personal foster chauffeur, would last before she started saying, 'You want to be driven into town *now*? Can't you see I'm *busy*?'

I said, 'Evelyn didn't like cars. For ecological reasons. Same here.'

Anyway, I didn't need Wendy's ideas for spending money. I had an excellent plan of my own. I told Bob about it.

'You want to have *dinner*?' he said. 'Don't you get enough food here?' He was half joking. Only half. He was worried I might be hungry.

160

I said, 'I mean, a special posh kind of dinner. When I invite people.'

'In a restaurant?'

'Bigger than that. In a big hall.'

'You mean, a banquet?'

'Yes.'

'OK. Tell me when you're ready and I'll see how I can help.'

Every night for a week, when I was trying not to fall asleep so I wouldn't pee myself, or after I'd peed myself when I couldn't get back to sleep, I planned it out and played it through in my mind. There'd be one hundred guests. Maybe more. There'd be a band. There'd be waiters in black suits carrying stuff around on trays. I'd invite everybody I'd ever known, specially anyone who'd been mean to me. Teachers who'd given me Detention. Boys from the year above who'd sneered and called me 'yellow scum'. The parking warden at the council Park-and-Ride who hated all of us from Bel'Vue.

There'd be dish after dish of fantastical foods, and drinks and sausages and desserts and chips and burgers, and at the end there'd be singing.

The band would play 'For he's a jolly good fellow'. They'd all be looking towards me sitting at the head of the great table. They'd be smiling with admiration because I was so rich and powerful and had offered them a feast.

I couldn't decide if I'd invite Daniel and Sharon and Miss Marshall, and Miss Marshall's friend Angie who I didn't know properly but who'd seemed quite nice. Sometimes they'd be there. Other times not. But every time I thought it through, right at the end, after the speeches when everybody was cheering me, there'd be the drone of bagpipes. A red curtain would swish open and Mrs McFee would come skipping in carrying a huge dish of deep-fried Mars bars and crooning her song, 'I belong to Glasgy and Glasgy belongs to me'.

The guests would titter, then laugh and jeer. Not at Mrs McFee, but at me.

So, no banquet.

Just as well. Because, next thing, I found out I wasn't going to get the money after all. I couldn't even go and look at it all piled up in the bank.

Wendy was a whole heap more disappointed than me. 'It's utterly absurd,' she said. 'They shouldn't be allowed to do this to him. Letting him down after all the build-up.'

I told her I was relieved. 'Being rich was very stressful.'

She rolled her eyes to the ceiling.

'Not that *you'd* know,' I added.

The World's My Oyster

Evelyn's money wasn't in gold bars. It was black printed figures on sheets of thick white paper.

I got a letter sent to me which I didn't understand.

Bob said, 'That'll be your statement.'

I said, 'No, it isn't.' A statement was what you had at school when you were a thicko. I'd got one of those already.

Bob said, 'That's a statement of special educational needs. This here's your bank statement.'

Bob did his best to explain it. The money was secured in a trust. That's why I couldn't spend it. It was controlled by stewards and trustees nominated on my behalf. It'd stay in the trust till I was eighteen, which was such a long way off it might as well have been never.

Bob said, 'It's not all bad news.' And he showed me how to look at the figures so they made sense. I could read numbers easier than words, specially if I knew which ones were the important ones.

'See, clear as daylight. Your pal's money safe as a rock. No leakage,' said Bob.

And it was getting to be more.

'That's your ethical investments,' Bob said. 'Must have been a canny old bird. So your trust gets interest and your financial adviser reinvests for you. Amazing, isn't it? Once you got money, it makes itself into more.'

Seeing all the big numbers made Wendy more determined than ever to get hold of them.

'On your behalf of course, pet. So you can enjoy what you're entitled to. It's only right.'

She soon found a way. She told Bob.

'This trust of his, it's educational. It's for if he wanted to go to university.'

I knew that'd never happen. So did Wendy. You have to be able to read long books with long words and no pictures. Kids from care don't go to university. Sharon told me.

'However, he's allowed to take some of the interest right away, so long as it's in his educational interest. One must find an objective which is of genuine educational benefit.'

I thought she might be planning to get me sent

away to a boarding school. But she had a very different kind of scam in mind for me.

'Travel is an education in itself, wouldn't you agree?' she said.

Bob scratched the back of his head and looked thoughtful. 'Affirmative,' he said.

She said, 'It broadens the mind. And some people's could definitely do with broadening.'

Soon the swirly sitting-room was covered in travel brochures. Florida, Venice, the Canadian Rockies, winter skiing, scuba diving, fjord cruises. Wendy flapped them in front of me, trying to get me to choose.

'There must be *somewhere* you'd like to visit,' she said.

Her travel talk was good because it took her mind off nagging me about dirty trainers on settee covers. And it was contagious. Eventually I began to get a feel for it, though I had my own idea about destinations. I decided to visit the village that had got the other half of the inheritance. I'd see how they were getting on with spending it. They were going to build a clinic. I wondered if they'd name it after her. 'The Evelyn Cairns Clinic' sounded good.

The village was in Colombia, in a rainforest.

When I told them, Wendy said, 'Jungle? Eek. Leeches, mosquitoes, no proper toilet facilities.'

Bob scratched his armpit as though mosquitoes were

inside his shirt syphoning off his blood. 'Hm, bit on the adventurous side,' he said and tried to find it on a map. But it was too small to be marked.

'Doesn't matter,' I said. 'I've changed my mind.' I'd realized that visiting a lost village wouldn't really work. Not because Bob couldn't find it, not because of Wendy or insects.

'It's something different,' I said, and told Bob about the trainee social workers who used to come to Bel'Vue to look at us. 'So, you see, I've been the sort of person that outsiders feel sorry for and wonder what to do about. There'll be boys in that village, maybe of my own age. I wouldn't want to stare at them as if they were exhibits any more than I used to like being stared at.'

Bob said, 'Yeah, I know what you mean.' But I didn't think he had a clue.

I said, 'Maybe if I'd learned the French from Daniel, then I could've talked to them and it wouldn't have been so hard.'

Wendy looked up from the airline timetable she was consulting. She said, 'It's not French they speak in Colombia. And we're going to some civilized places, where they'll speak English. Oooh, here's a good one. "California and the Golden West in ten days".'

I said, 'Wherever I go, you're coming too? On Evelyn's money?'

'*Your* money, pet. You know it's yours. And obviously you can't go travelling alone, can you? And if you're not comfortable with the notion, pet, you could try looking on it as a small gift of recompense. Your gift to us in return for our gift to you.'

'What gift?'

'We have offered you our home, haven't we? And so it's only natural that you'd want to return that gift in some way. And it's a lovely and thoughtful way you're choosing to do it. We both think it's really sweet of you, pet. A lovely gesture on your part.'

I wasn't yet adopted, so they couldn't take me anywhere without permission from Social Services. Wendy applied for it and soon got it. She and the new social worker were becoming thick as thieves.

'I've heard of similar schemes with young offenders. They're taken on camping hikes to Spain. They benefit enormously,' said the social worker.

Wendy explained that her latest idea was much more adventurous. 'It's to be a once-in-a-lifetime, round-the-world trip.'

The social worker thought that an equally splendid project, even if there wouldn't be any camping involved. 'It'll really help him find himself. Perhaps you should take in Hong Kong.'

Wendy agreed. 'The travel agent says the shopping there is second to none.'

'I meant, more so Mak can consolidate the work my predecessor was doing on his ethnic-identity awareness.'

I didn't bother to remind her that I was born in Cardiff.

'And, whatever else happens,' said the social worker, 'it'll be a great bonding experience for you all.'

The special-support teacher at school thought it was a good idea, too. 'Learning through doing,' she said. She gave me a new notebook from the stationery cupboard and told me I must write something in it every day.

'Even if it's only a line or two. It'll be like your travel journal. I'll expect you to bring it to me when you get back.'

So, instead of spending the first day of the holidays felt-tipping rude words on the bathroom wall, as I'd planned, I was in a 747 climbing up through the air. At 18,000 feet, the aircraft turned east towards Dover and continued to climb. And after Dover came France, and then Italy.

We were in row number 40, side by side in seats A, B and C. We were wearing matching jogging suits, shiny mauve with a green flash down the sleeve, which Wendy said were ideal apparel for any long-haul trip.

I felt a complete idiot.

I opened the support teacher's notebook. I was going to ask Bob to help me with spelling, but he had his eyes shut so I had to do it by myself.

On the first page I wrote, 'DAY ONE. left Heathrow 16.30 hrs. going east.' Then I flipped to the back of the notebook and on the last page I wrote, 'DAY 23. left New YorK. arived safley back Heathrow. Touchdown 15.45 hrs. school tomorow.'

I hoped I'd have enough stuff to fill in the rest of the days.

AIRBORNE

Flight QA 082

They had their first big row in Rome. I didn't even know we were going to Rome. But, since I didn't know what Rome, or any other foreign city, might look like, it didn't make any difference to me where we went.

'It's a twenty-four-hour stopover,' said Bob as we queued at the passport desk.

'Rome is an important city to know about,' Wendy said. 'See Rome and die, that's what they say. Once you've seen it, you can write it up in your little notebook, can't you?'

See Rome and shriek, it should've been. That's what she did almost as soon as we'd been shown up to our rooms at the hotel. I could hear her through the wall.

I'd never been inside a hotel before. This one was brilliant. My room had two huge beds, as springy as a pair of trampolines. I could throw myself from one to the other without touching the floor. There was a basket of fruit with a neat card saying 'Welcome' stuck in it. There was a fridge disguised as a cupboard and filled with cold drinks, dry-roasted peanuts, Swiss chocolate, and one Mars bar. I had my own bathroom with free shampoo, soap, bath bubbles and shaving stuff. There was a film channel on the telly that showed films round the clock, all day, all night. I found a swimming pool on the hotel roof which I could use any time. I just had to give my room number to the pool attendant.

I was the only person wandering around the Via Appia Antica Hotel in a shiny mauve jogging suit. But I didn't mind. The doorman held open the glass entrance door for me just as if I was a well-dressed adult. And when I came back two minutes later, after looking at the two exotic palm trees outside, he smiled as though the one thing he wanted to do with his life was open and close the door for me.

I'd have stayed in that hotel for all the twenty-three days if only Wendy hadn't got a busy round-the-world schedule.

While I was in mid-air, flinging myself from one power-spring bed to the other, I suddenly thought of Evelyn. I hoped she could see me and knew how happy I was. I was happier than I had ever been in my entire life.

The shouting from the next door stopped. Wendy

came into my room. She told me it was time to go out and look at Rome. Not her. Just Bob and me. She stayed behind and sulked. I thought, Bit of a waste coming all this way. But I didn't say so.

Bob and I walked to some ruins. They were supposed to be very special. Neither of us knew why. We watched some stray cats frolicking among the old stone pillars and I wondered about Mr Twitchett. Then we went and had some ice cream.

At the hotel, I went back to my brilliant room to do some more trampolining. The arguing started again. I didn't know what it was about but I could hear his voice rumbling through the wall, then hers yelling, then both of them at once.

Then it went silent, as though they'd both died or killed each other. I thought about that for a while and what I'd do if they had. The silence went on. I heard their door click as though one of them was going out. Then it clicked again, so whichever one it was must have come back in. I went up to the pool on the roof and as there weren't any other people needing anything, the attendant showed me how to do the back-stroke. He can't have known I was a kid from care or he wouldn't have wasted so much time on me.

I didn't see any more of them that evening and we never got to have any supper. Just as well Bob and I had

had the ice creams earlier. I ate all the stuff there was in the fridge. (Except the beer and whisky. Mira once told me that my biological father's troubles were all due to drinking. I didn't want to be like him.)

The Mars bar was so cold it didn't taste of anything.

I didn't get another decent meal until we were 25,000 feet up in the air flying over Greece. I know it was Greece because the pilot told us over the intercom. So I wrote it in the notebook: 'DAY 3. 25,000 feet. Greece. Seat A'.

The air food was brilliant. It was on a tray that fitted on to a neat flap-down table in front of you. Everything was wrapped up like it was a brand-new present, even the salt and sugar and spoons and forks. Not like in the school canteen where the cutlery is on an open tray for anybody to spit on as they go past.

I liked being on the aircraft. I'd have been happy to stay in it and just keep flying round and round the earth.

Bob and Wendy should've been enjoying themselves too, because the stewards came along offering out drinks several times. They could've had as much wine as they wanted. But they didn't seem to be in a mood for fun. It was a waste of them being there, specially as I didn't need them to look after me. Cabin staff did it. I pressed a buzzer over my seat and they'd bring me a can of

fizzy, or some crisps, or a pillow. One of them brought
me a map that showed our flight path.

If Social Services replaced all its care staff with airline
cabin staff, they'd have kids queuing up to be admitted
to dumps like Bel'Vue.

Bob sweated a lot, specially during take-off. I could
see it bubbling up on his neck under his scraggy beard.
He sighed a lot, too, as though he couldn't breathe.

Wendy told him off. 'Oh, do stop it,' she snapped.

I was sitting by the window. But after we'd had our
second meal, she made me move to sit in seat B in the
middle of the row. I thought it was so she could have a
turn looking out of the window. But she put on the
black eye-mask they give you and went to sleep. Or
pretended to. You couldn't tell with the mask on. She
only changed places so she wouldn't be sitting next to
him. But I didn't like having to sit between them like a
boundary fence.

So I got up and squeezed past Bob's knees and moved
to a row where there were two empty seats. You weren't
meant to move about. One of the stewards came over
to see if I was all right.

'Good on ya, sport,' he said and put up the arm-rests
so I could lie down. Then he brought a blanket and
tucked me in.

We got to Hong Kong early in the morning. I didn't know what to expect.

As we came roaring down through thick clouds towards the spiky mountain-tops, I suddenly saw the islands and the silver-grey water below, and the skyscrapers sticking up like bristles, and I felt massively excited. I definitely hadn't planned to feel anything. I'd warned myself not to have any feelings at all.

But the new social worker had been right all along. She'd said it was going to be an important turning-point for the three of us. And it was, though not in the way she meant.

Pearl of the Orient

It was six o'clock when we landed. They weren't feeling too good. They looked like sick people getting over the flu. Both were grumbling.

'Could be Wales,' said Bob. 'Easily.'

'Whales?' I said. 'Where? I can't see any.'

'No, Wales. Looks like it. Grey sky. All those hills. Just needs a few sheep.'

We had to queue for immigration control. It took longer than at Rome.

'Do stop jumping up and down like that,' she snapped. 'You're only drawing attention to us.'

There were Chinese police, or perhaps they were soldiers, standing in groups watching the passengers coming off the aircraft. I thought it was exciting.

'Don't forget, these are communists,' Wendy said. 'They're armed.'

The armed Chinese looked uninterested in us in our

crumpled jogging suits. It was a businessman in the queue behind they took aside. I thought that was exciting too.

I said, 'I wonder if he's smuggling something.'

Wendy said, 'Oh, do be quiet, can't you?'

The Pearl of the Orient Hotel we were taken to seemed very dark for a pearl. Wendy didn't like it.

'You booked it, dear,' said Bob.

'So how was I to know it'd be like this? I've never been to China before.'

'We none of us have, sweetheart,' said Bob. He'd never called her 'sweetheart' before. I knew it was a bad sign.

'You know it wasn't me that did the booking. You know it was Sheryl at the agency.'

Our room was on the twenty-fourth floor. Wendy didn't like that, either. She was probably right. It was very small so we couldn't move about easily. Everything in it was brown. There was a heavy blind over the window so you couldn't look out, and a noisy electric hum from the ceiling.

'Twin beds!' said Wendy. 'I don't believe it.'

The two beds were side by side. Wendy got very upset.

'I'm going to phone reception,' she said.

But that didn't help.

'They're talking Chinese to me,' she muttered through her clenched teeth.

Bob didn't believe her. 'They can't be,' he said. 'Not in a four-star hotel.'

'Well, it definitely sounded like Chinese to me,' she said.

She didn't understand them. But they understood her, because a Chinese steward in hotel uniform came to the room. He pulled out a small bed from under one of the others.

'This roll-away bed, madam,' he said with a bow but no smile.

It was already made up with sheets and a pillow. It was meant for me.

Wendy said, 'I have booked two rooms.'

'This one room, madam. You have one room booked.' He opened the door and pointed to the number on the outside.

'I don't mind sharing,' I said, even though I did because it meant I wouldn't be able to do any trampolining.

Bob fiddled with the air-conditioning control so it wouldn't make such a hum. Wendy rolled the roll-away bed back under the bed. Then we went to the hotel buffet for breakfast. First breakfast for them. Second breakfast for me, because I'd already had the one on the 747.

Wendy didn't like the look of the food spread out on the buffet counter. I don't think Bob did either but he didn't say anything, just took a pot of tea.

'It's all Chinese,' Wendy said.

The Chinese tea was a strange colour and smelled of seaweed. There were chilli spiced noodles, slimy things like fungus floating in pondwater, and a pan of something white and red. Several other people were helping themselves to it. I asked the steward what it was.

'Kop daei chuk, sir,' he said.

'I don't know what that is,' I said. I was very polite.

'Pig-organ congee, sir,' he said with a bow.

Wendy made a Maisie-sick face. I took a big helping anyway and some spicy noodles. I said, 'Now we're here, we might as well make the most of it.'

I went back for a second helping of the congee. I saw there was other food too. Croissants, cereals, bacon and eggs on a hot plate under a lid.

Wendy still hadn't taken anything. Bob fetched her some orange juice. He said, 'Wendy's got a touch of jet-lag.'

I said, 'There's plenty of ordinary food. Bacon and beans and stuff. If you want it.'

'Ergh. How could anybody even think of fried bacon at this time of day?'

They soon went back to the room. I went to the top of the building to look for the swimming pool. But there was no pool. Up on the flat roof I found a thatched shack with a television aerial and washing hanging off it. Some people seemed to be living there. The woman was squatting beside a small fire and stirring something in a sizzling pan. I went back down in the lift to our level.

They must've been having another of their fights. I felt elastic tightness in the room like a storm that had gone away but was soon coming back to churn everything up some more.

There were muffled splashings from the bathroom. That was him. She was lying rigid on one of the beds with the airline mask over her eyes.

'There isn't a pool here,' I said. 'D'you know if there'll be one at the next hotel?'

I couldn't remember where we were supposed to be going after Hong Kong. But I reckoned I'd discovered three important things about travelling – the eating, the flying and the swimming.

She didn't reply. I put on the telly.

'Don't,' she said, not moving.

'OK,' I said and zapped speedily through news in Chinese, sport in Chinese, singing in Chinese and Chinese straight-talking. I couldn't understand any of them. I switched off. I crept round the foot of her bed, pressing myself against the wall so I wouldn't disturb her.

'What d'you think you're doing?'

How did she know I was doing anything? She must've been peeking under the mask.

'Going to look out the window. All right by you? Or do I need written permission?'

I climbed on to the window recess. But I couldn't make the blind roll up. Then I realized it wasn't meant to. It was fixed. The window wasn't made to open either. I managed to haul up the bottom edge of the blind and I saw why they'd blanked out the view. There wasn't anything you'd call a view.

The next building was so close you could almost reach across to it. It was streaky grey and green like it was growing mould on the side, and every window was barred, even on the top storeys. There was washing pegged to some of the window bars.

I knew a bit about nicking things. Only a very desperate thief, or a mad one, would climb up a thirty-storey building to break in.

I could see in through the window of the nearest flat. It looked like a kitchen. I saw a fridge with a mega telly on top, and on the telly a mega electric fan. An old woman, dried up like the monkey grandmother, was rolling something out on a wooden board. A man in a vest sat at the same table smoking and reading a newspaper. A baby was sitting on the table too, and the man kept one arm out to stop it slipping off. A younger woman was at the table ironing.

A boy in shorts sat up on the window ledge, cross-legged. Perhaps that was the only place left. Perhaps the bars weren't to stop thieves getting in but children from falling out. The boy seemed to be doing homework. He glanced up and saw me watching him across the gap. He went on looking at me for so long that I had to turn away.

Bob came out of the shower, wet and fat in a bath-towel.

He said, 'Did you have a swim?'

'It isn't that kind of hotel.' I didn't mention the woman doing her stir-fry on top of the roof. Wendy might have got in a panic about the fire risks.

Bob peered over my shoulder. 'Long way down,' he said. 'Wouldn't like to jump.'

'You couldn't. The window's fixed.'

We stared down at the ground far below. There were some tiny people like Lego men, dressed in red, with red flags. Some were drumming. I thought they might be soldiers, though they weren't marching, just moving in a strange way.

'Religious guys, wouldn't you say?' Bob said. 'Doing some sort of holy festival thing?'

'Oh. Are they?' It felt weird not understanding what I was looking down at. 'I thought they must be army people.'

At the base of the tower block there was a patch of park. Another group of people, old ones this time, were doing something else, all together, slowly moving in a sort of dance. It looked as though they were floating, though I knew they couldn't really.

I got them wrong, too.

Bob said, 'That's t'ai chi.'

'Who?'

'One of the martial arts. An exercise for combat.'

Ancient wrinklies. Not floating, but fighting.

Wendy suddenly sat up and pulled off her eye-mask. 'Get down off there!' she said.

Bob said, 'He likes being up there.'

'He'll give himself vertigo.'

'No he won't.' Then, to me, he said, 'Look, there's a boy over there.'

'I know.'

'You could almost be him, couldn't you?'

I'd already thought of that. 'No I couldn't. No way.'

'Same age, same everything.'

'I've never lived in a skyscraper flat. I've never had a baby sister.'

Bob waved across to the boy. He didn't wave back. Of course he didn't. We were just foreign tourists gazing stupidly out of a hotel window.

'Close that blind, can't you?' Wendy snapped. 'We don't need the whole world gawping in.'

I didn't take any notice. She picked up her travel case and went into the bathroom. She closed the door firmly. She locked it. I thought, If only she could be persuaded to stay in there all the time. Even sleep in there.

We'd only been in Room 531 for a few hours. Already I felt suffocated. What was it like for the neighbours across the chasm, all of them squashed into their sweaty kitchen for ever and ever?

I said to Bob, 'What are we going to do next?'

He said, 'We'll wait till Wendy's ready. See what she'd like. Seems there's plenty of choice.'

He picked a coloured leaflet off the bedside shelf.

' "Hong Kong, City of Life",' he read and tossed it over to me. 'See for yourself. Trips, trams, zoos, cinemas, museums. It's all here. Take your pick.'

When Wendy came out of the bathroom, she definitely looked ready to go somewhere. She'd changed out of her jogging suit into normal clothes. She had one bag over her shoulder, and her travel case in her hand.

She slapped the airline tickets on to the bed. 'Yours,' she said. 'And his.' She tapped her handbag. 'Mine.'

'What d'you mean?' said Bob.

I let the blind drop with a thump. But I stayed up on the window recess.

'I'm taking the next flight. Don't try and come too.'

'Wendy, sweetheart.'

'There isn't room for the three of us. I'm going home.'

Bob scrambled over the bed towards her. 'Wait. Please. I'll go down and ask again. I'm sure they can find us an extra room if I insist.'

She said, 'You know exactly what I mean. It isn't anything about hotel rooms.'

I knew what she meant. That there wasn't room in life for the three of us to be together.

I thought of explaining this to him. But decided it wasn't the moment. She avoided looking at me. He went to take her luggage from her.

'No I can do it. I'll call a taxi in reception.'

I wondered how she'd manage that when she kept complaining she couldn't understand anybody.

'Wendy. Please wait.'

'You're not to come down with me.'

How could he? He was only wearing boxer shorts.

They both went out into the corridor and closed the door so I couldn't see them. I couldn't hear them either. If they were talking, they were keeping their voices down.

City of Life

He came back in alone.

He sat on the edge of the bed with his head in his hands. That seemed odd. They'd been arguing so much that I thought he ought to be relieved she'd finally pushed off.

I thought, She might at least have bothered to say goodbye.

He began to mutter into his hands so I couldn't hear properly.

'What?' I said.

'She meant it. She's always meant it. She's been telling me for years.'

I said, 'Is it because of me?' I wasn't intending to say sorry. I just wanted to know.

He said, 'Of course not. There were cracks long before you turned up. You're the cement that was going to hold us together.'

I remembered Evelyn once saying I was like the piece of seaweed in her life. I wasn't sure which was worse. To be cement that didn't stick or washed-up seaweed.

I said, 'My biological father did that to my biological mother. You know, walked out on her. It made her mad. That's why she dumped me.'

I wondered how long it'd be before Bob dumped me. If he did, I wasn't sure what I'd do. I didn't even know if they had Social Services. They might place me with a Chinese foster family. I wouldn't understand what anybody was saying. I'd get very upset and angry. And if I was made to go to school, I wouldn't be able to read even the easy things because of the Chinese way of writing being so different. It was an awesome thought.

I remembered Daniel saying you'd got to hang on to anybody you'd got, however lousy they were.

'Bob?' I said.

He didn't answer.

I was going to ask if he'd hang on till we were back before he dumped me because I didn't fancy my chances in a school where the writing was in Chinese. But he suddenly let out a low groan, rolled over on the bed, pulled the sheet up over his head and started sobbing. After a while it turned into howling. It was like Maisie all over again. Like me, too.

I knew ice cubes didn't work. I let him get on with it by himself. His marriage wasn't my problem. His howling under the sheet wasn't half as annoying as both of them arguing.

I turned on the telly. I watched a programme about wildlife in mainland China. I didn't understand a word but the animals looked interesting. Daniel once told me that in China people ate any kind of living creature, including dogs and sea slugs.

While Sobbing-Bob got on with his howl, I fiddled around the room, tidied the stuff in my bum-bag and wondered about taking a shower. The room being so small, there wasn't scope for many activities.

When he'd stopped making a noise, and was just lying there staring at the air-conditioning panel on the ceiling, I said, 'We better go out for a walk since we're here.'

He got up without saying anything. I handed him his jogging pants. He put them on. Then his trainers. He put them on. I picked up the plastic key-card for the room and put it in my pocket. I went to the door. He followed. I walked to the lift. He was still there, just behind me. It was like taking a large daft dog for a walk. Or else a small dumb donkey.

When we reached street level, I said, 'You OK, then?'

He nodded. But he didn't really look as though he

was feeling anything, good, bad or middling. It was like he'd been clonked on the head by a 747, fully loaded, and lost his memory.

We walked for hours. Along the big wide pavements with the bright smart shops full of clothes and computers just like the ones at home, past fountains and statues and parks. We looked at the grey sea, at the grey ships, at the choppy grey waves slapping against the jetty wall. I felt seasick.

We went on walking and got to streets that were all Chinese. We passed small corners with incense sticks burning and flowers stuck in rusty yellow milk tins. And there were food stalls, and open-fronted shops selling dried snakes, octopuses, spices, dark powders, creatures that looked like babies' hands, and dried seahorses by the basketful.

I said, 'What d'you think they do with them?'

Bob said, glumly, 'Supposed to be special, seahorses, aren't they? The males get the eggs, fertilize them, take care of the young. The females just go off, swim away.'

I said, 'But what are they for? Do they eat them?'

'Expect they think they're an aphrodisiac.'

'What's that mean?'

But he'd gone silent again, chin down, not seeming to see anything. It was like he was walking blind. I saw things. I was looking out all the time, trying to find the way back. I saw people look at me. Their eyes were inspecting my face. What is he? Is he one of us? Or isn't he?

I walked close to him. I didn't intend to. Close enough to be touching. I needed to feel him there. Big slob Bob like a greasy mountain. He'd protect me against these staring people.

A thousand thousand eyes peeking at me, to see who I was. I didn't know. I knew I didn't want to be Welsh. But I didn't want to be Chinese either. I wanted to be me.

A thunderstorm was coming. We heard the cracking and banging. I thought we'd be OK because tropical rain's supposed to be warm.

But it wasn't. It was as cold as any other kind of rain.

I said, 'It must be Welsh rain.' I wanted to make him laugh. I failed.

The wise Chinese people on the pavement had umbrellas or else they were sheltering under the awnings of their shops. All except the beggars. But even the beggars had plastic covers over their heads.

I was glad when we finally made it back to the Pearl of the Orient Hotel. We were both soaked through. Bob hadn't said another word and was shivering.

'You better take a shower,' I said. 'To warm up.'

We were too late to have a meal.

The manager said, 'Restaurant closed now, sir.' He was very polite. I liked being called 'sir'. I liked being bowed to.

'Maybe we could have some sandwiches or chips or something?'

The manager nodded politely. 'Room service. Regret too late now, sir. Hotel kitchen closed. Breakfast six thirty, ten o'clock. Maybe you go find hot food in dai poi dong, sir.'

'What?'

'Dai poi dong, sir, cook food centre, open very late, sir.'

I went back up to the room. I felt a failure but not as big a failure as Bob felt. He handed me a piece of folded paper. It was a note, written on Pearl of the Orient Hotel paper.

'Found it, just now,' he mumbled.

It had 'Mak' on the front. I opened it out. But it was too scribbly. I handed it back.

He read it out to me.

Mak, I am *sorry* it has to end like this. But it was bound not to work out. The social worker said it was only a fifty-fifty chance. Your passport's in Robert's jacket pocket. And the rest of the dollars. I'll pay you back *every last penny of your money* that's been spent on my ticket *as soon as* you return. Tell Robert I'll be *moving out*. He knows where. Yrs, Wendy.

I checked the two tickets still lying on the bed beside Bob. Figures are easier than words. We had to check in for our next flight two hours before take-off. They always made you do that. Then you had to stay in the departure lounge watching a screen to see when the number for your flight showed. Wendy and Bob hated the waiting about. I didn't. It was part of the travelling.

'Listen Bob,' I said. 'I'm sorry about no food. But as soon as we're on our next flight they're bound to give us a meal. Can you last till then?'

He shrugged, lay down and slept just where he was. I suppose he had jet-lag too. He hadn't bothered to take a shower. I took his trainers off. They were very smelly.

I could've slept on the other bed. But supposing she changed her mind and came back? It was a million to one chance but it wasn't worth the risk.

I pulled out the roll-away bed. I was muddled as to whether it was daytime or night. That's what jet-lag does to you. But I didn't intend to sleep much anyway. I had to make sure I was awake in time for us to catch the airport express.

Bob and I were ready and waiting on the front steps

of the Pearl of the Orient. There was a tropical drizzle falling. The airport bus swished towards us. I was dead chuffed to see it.

I thought, If this was where my roots were supposed to be, I didn't want anything more to do with them.

I thought I'd almost rather be back with the old roots. But that was only because I didn't yet know about putting down new roots.

Good on Ya, Sport

I liked the take-offs, hearing the engines roaring. Moving slowly forward, feeling the thundering power held only just in check.

I liked the way the aircraft pounded down the runway like a heavy bird that has to run like heck to get airborne. I liked the surge of speed and the force of gravity pressing you back into your seat till you felt you could hardly breathe.

I liked looking down at the toy world disappearing till inside the cabin was the only real place.

I liked the way every passenger had their own spotlamp over their seat, their own personal control pad and headphones for the music channels. I liked the way the stewards kept smiling and brought children their meal trays first.

On each flight, they gave us each a bag of small presents. Like a Christmas stocking back at Bel'Vue.

Sensible, safe and non-personal things. Quiz books, jigsaws, comics, toy cars.

I got pencils with a wildlife colouring book. It was meant for children years younger than me. But to some people I've always seemed small for my age.

I flicked through the pictures. Then I read what it said underneath each creature. If I went slowly, it wasn't too difficult.

' "Spot the hopping kangaroo. An adult can cover more than nine metres in one leap." '

Wow!

' "See the cuddly koala ride upon its mother's back." '

Aaah!

' "Listen to the laughing kookaburra." '

Tee-hee!

No prizes for guessing our next stop. Airline Santa Claus is getting us ready.

I started to colour them in crazy ways. Pink koala, purple turtle, green possum. Then I came to the emu. I knew about the emu. It was crazy colours anyway. Daniel had put up that poster in our bedroom. The skin of its face is blue, and so is its neck. I scribbled away with the pencils. I did its long legs in multicolour like striped stockings.

One of the stewards came past. He saw the stripy

emu. 'Say, that's a real beaut!' he said. 'Not many of them around!'

I was going to colour in the rest of them, the kookaburra red, the wombat spotty, but then I had a better idea.

If I put all this stuff into the travel journal I'd use up loads of pages.

Carefully I began to copy out some of the words so it'd look as though I'd thought them up myself.

' "The emu is a large flightless bird. But it can run at a speed of 48 kilometres per hour." '

I knew that already, so it was easy to copy.

' "It lives in small mobs. The female lays the eggs. They weigh 1 kilo each. The male incubates them. The male cares for the chicks." '

What a crazy bird.

When I'd seen to the rest, more than half the pages of the notebook looked filled. Brilliant. The special-support teacher would be pleased.

The chatty steward came back. 'Looks like your old man's all clapped out, so d'you fancy coming to have a Captain Cook in the flight deck?'

'He's not my old man,' I started to say. But I swallowed it. 'OK,' I said. 'Sure.'

The pilot had a broad smile which showed big shiny teeth.

'How're ya going?' he said.

So I said, 'She's apples.' That's what the steward had said to me earlier. I told the pilot I was enjoying the flight, that I liked the film and the food, and the only thing I wasn't sure about was what we were going to do when we arrived at our next stop.

He laughed. He said, 'If you've any sense, you'll head off to spend the arvo on the beach with the rest of the surfies.' Then he explained what some of the lighted dials meant. There wasn't anything to see out of the front except space and the flashing dot of another aircraft far away on the purple horizon.

The aircraft was flown mostly by computers.

'No worries, sport,' he said.

The steward brought him some tea and took me back to my place.

I used to think that if I could get up into the sky above the clouds, I'd somehow be nearer Evelyn, and even if I couldn't see her she'd see me. But if she saw me now, she'd have to see Bob too. And he wasn't an attractive sight.

He was awake. Sweat was pouring off him like rain off a Welsh hillside.

I tried to ignore him. But his fat, pink sausage fingers were clutching the arm-rests. He had his eyes fixed on the 'No smoking' panel just above our heads. Perhaps he thought it'd change its words to give him a new message.

I said, 'What's up with you now?'

He opened his mouth to speak but no words came out. I tried to explain to him why we were safer up here than down there, because of it being a closed world, where nothing real could get at you and nobody could tell you what you had to be. But he didn't seem to understand.

I said, 'Still scared?'

He nodded.

'What of?'

He didn't seem to know.

I said, 'If it's crashing you're scared of, we won't. It's all done by computers.'

He shook his head.

'Dying, then? No? Not dying. Staying alive? Existing? Everything? Well, you've probably forgotten something. We're supposed to be on a trip of a lifetime. So it's time to lighten up.'

He looked rough. Fat, sweaty, tired, with his lank hair sitting on his neck. I'd always hated that greasy ponytail more than the belly.

I said, 'I know what. I'll do a deal with you. If we get down to earth again, will you get rid of your rat's tail?'

His hand moved involuntarily up to touch it, to

check it was still alive. He shrugged.

I said, 'I'll take that as a "Yes". We'll shake on it.' His hand was very damp.

I gave him my travel journal. I said, 'And if you haven't anything else to do, maybe you'd check the spelling. I've got to give it in when we get back.'

I didn't really care about my spelling. But I thought it might take his mind off his suffering.

From seat A, row 15, 30,000 feet up, the largest island in the world was reddish, sometimes with bumps and shadows, creases and ruffles which might have been gullies and creeks and might not. I couldn't see any of the sheep, or trees, or fences or first people. It was mostly desert.

Wendy said a growing boy needed space. She thought a sun lounge would be enough.

Evelyn said Australia's got more space than it's got sheep or gum trees, stretching away as far as you can see, to the edge of the earth. That was just the kind of space I'd like. Staring at it put me into a dream. For hours and kilometres I slept.

I missed the film. I missed the next meal tray. I didn't wake till the stewards were telling us to return our seats to the upright position, to fasten our safety belts and to prepare for descent.

Coming down with the roaring in our ears, Bob got

scared again. He shut his eyes and gripped the arm-rests so tightly his hands went white.

I said, 'D'you reckon we've reached the end of the world and we're going to fall off the edge? OK, don't answer then. Just look out the window. Isn't it brilliant?'

Now it was green. There were rivers. And the sea was felt-tip blue with a frill of white where it touched the coastline.

I said, 'Even if he overshoots the runway, he can land on the water, except it's probably seething with ravenous sharks.'

Bob didn't think that was funny.

After Immigration, we waited and waited in the hall where the baggage arrives after it's been unloaded. It took a long time to find out that ours was missing. It'd gone on to Tasmania or New Zealand. They weren't sure which. Either way, they said, it'd take a while to get it back. At least a couple of days, maybe longer.

They issued us with special vouchers so we could buy basic things like toothbrushes.

'No worries. Enjoy your stay,' the airline clerk said.

It sounded as though luggage quite often got flown on to somewhere else.

Bob didn't seem bothered. In fact, he seemed relieved to have lost all his stuff.

'Less to carry,' he said, 'while we check our bearings.'

Southern Hemisphere

We took the airline bus to the city. The driver was Greek. He dropped us off right near the central harbour. We went to an Italian café where we could watch the green ferries chugging in and out. Bob had a coffee. The waitress, who told us she was from Croatia, called it a flat-top. I had a pineapple milkshake. The cashier, who was a Scot, called it a smoothie.

Bob said, 'Seems easy enough to pick up the lingo.'

We watched the passengers, all shapes, colours, sizes, sauntering off the incoming ferries, strolling on to the outgoing ones. Nobody was frowning. Nobody was yelling. Nobody was staring at anybody as if to tell them they didn't belong. Round here it seemed everybody belonged, even if they came from somewhere else.

From the café we could see the massive curved bridge reaching across the harbour to the coast on the far side. It was loads bigger than it'd looked on Evelyn's tea towel. The sailing boats going under looked the same.

Bob and I had nothing to do except to pass the time in any way we chose. We got ferry tickets and followed the crowd with the beach gear. We sat way up front. It was like that time on top of the double-decker bus in London with Evelyn. Bob was looking less gloomy by the hour, like he was prepared to be on holiday at last. I was too. We'd made it to the other side of the world.

I said, 'D'you know about déjà vu?'

'Try me.'

'My friend Daniel said it's when something happens and you almost feel it's happened before. That's what I feel now, like I've seen all this before.'

And in a way I had, even if it was only on a tea towel.

Bob grinned and winked. 'Well, I can tell you straight, *I've* never seen all this before. It's all new to me.'

'It's famous, that bridge,' I told him. 'All over the world. It's a symbol for leaving and arriving.'

Now I really did feel nearer to Evelyn than ever before. But I didn't miss her. I was glad she wasn't here. She'd have had to tell me everything about this country. I didn't want to be told. I wanted us to find out for ourselves, Bob and me, together.

The ferry chugged across the harbour, into the dark-blue shade under the bridge, out again to sunlight.

Bob pointed up. 'Hey, look at that! They're crazy!'

There were people like white ants walking in single file along the topmost curve of the iron bridge. They were linked together by a rope like mountain climbers, so if one of them should slip the others would hold them.

Evelyn had told me she'd wanted to do that, on her last visit back. But she hadn't been brave enough.

Weird or what? She'd been brave enough to think about me and the Colombians even when she knew she was dying. I wondered if I'd ever get to be that brave. Or maybe I'd had the chance and let it slip by without noticing.

Bob and I made our way to a beach by tagging along behind a gang of boys with surfboards over their shoulders.

We found hot golden sand with white splashy surf, and strong-looking lifeguards in straw sun hats keeping watch through binoculars on everybody in the water.

Scattered over the beach were pine cones and seaweed, and all types of people. Some were on their own, some in families, some with iceboxes full of beer, some with sunshades and babies in buggies, and grannies and picnics. There was plenty of room for all sorts, though in the water they had to swim in the right place or the lifeguards blew whistles and yelled through a loudhailer, 'Keep between the flags!'

It was warm inside our long-sleeved jogging suits. At least we matched, so if anybody thought we looked out of place they'd have to stare at both of us. But nobody did, though a woman with some children offered me a turn with her tube of sunblock.

'Hey, you need some of this?' she said.

Perhaps she could see we were new. Perhaps she could see that Bob was already turning red.

'Thanks,' I said. I put some on his nose. He put some on mine. Then we moved to sit in the shade of one of the pine trees. We watched the ocean rollers crashing in, the bathers wallowing like porpoises, and the surfers skimming in like they were speeding over ice. It looked more skilled than flying.

A doddery old couple came and settled on the sand near us. They slowly unpacked a picnic and ate it with chopsticks out of small cardboard boxes. Their food and their faces looked Chinese, but when they spoke to each other you could tell they were real Australians.

Even in the shade of the pine tree, Bob and I were getting too hot. I rolled up the legs of my jogging trousers. I said, 'We ought to go in the water. To cool down.'

'Not got any bathing trunks.'

'We could go in our boxers and dry off in the sun?'

'No thanks. Not me.'

'Oh, come on.'

'Don't feel like it. Too rough.'

'That's the whole point. It's fun. Look, there's even little kids out there.'

When they were knocked over by a big roller, they got up all spluttering and ran towards the waves for more. You knew it was all right because the lifeguards were there watching and ready to dive in.

I tried to pull Bob up.

He kept making excuses. 'No, Mak. No way!' he said.

In a way he was right, because we hadn't got any other clothes to change into except what we were wearing. Our mauve jogging suits, our underclothes, our smelly socks and our smelly trainers. Everything else was halfway to Hobart or Wellington.

Eventually I managed to force him to take off his trainers and come for a paddle. We dashed fast over the burning beach. We reached the strange sea which was greenish-blue like a glass bottle you could see right through. The small waves rippled round our feet and washed little stones between our toes. But when a wave came running towards us almost like a long low animal that was alive, Bob clutched on to me as though he thought he was drowning.

The water was warm and only up to his ankles. It couldn't possibly drown him. It was weird. Scared of flying. Scared of water. What else was he scared of?

'Just those two,' he said. 'So would you be if you couldn't swim.'

I didn't believe him. 'Course you can swim! Everybody knows how to!'

Bob shook his head.

'You *sure*?'

'Never had anybody to teach me.'

'*I'll* teach you.' I only meant it as a joke.

He took it seriously. 'OK. Tomorrow. If we find a calm enough place and if I pluck up courage.'

'Yes. Between the two flags, where the lifeguards are watching.'

He said, 'I'll need to learn, won't I? I'll never pass for a real Australian if I can't even swim.'

'How d'you mean, "real"?'

'We're planning on staying, aren't we?'

'Staying?'

'That's what I said.'

'You mean properly stay? Like never go away?'

'Who knows? Never's a long time.'

'But, like, live here longer than a couple of weeks? Like we were real Aussies?'

'Well, you won't catch me going up in one of those 747 contraptions again.'

Weird geezer. Still couldn't see the fun of flying.

I said, 'Just the two of us?'

'I haven't anyone else in mind. Have you?'

'No.' I thought of telling him about the emu. The seahorse, too, but specially the emu. Instead, I told him about Evelyn's grandparents, sailing round the world to settle forever in a place they knew nothing about, and waiting a year to get a plot where they could build their wooden home.

It hadn't been easy back then. It might not be easy for us either. I said, 'Bob, there's loads of stuff we'd have to do.'

He blinked. 'Stuff? What d'you mean, "stuff"?'

'Important stuff.' I searched in my mind for that word Daniel had taught me. I reckoned I found it.

'Legislations,' I said.

Bob blinked thoughtfully.

'You know, the paperwork, filling in forms. You can't move into somebody's country just like that, without them wanting to check you out.' I thought, And it'll probably be like being got ready for adoption. Hours of dreary meetings and talking and file cards covered in scribbled notes.

Bob sighed. 'Sure, it'd be a hassle, but that doesn't

mean we shouldn't give it a try, does it?'

I said, 'We'll need to find ourselves a lawyer. My friend Daniel said with a good lawyer you can do anything you like. Even change your identity. But you only have to do that if you've done something really bad and you're on the run.'

'We won't need to change our identities. I'll be me and you'll be you. But we'll be Australians.'

'*If* they let us stay,' I added. For a few moments, I was the cautious one. Bob was the cheery kid peering into an easy future. He said, 'It would be good if we could find ourselves a place with a backyard. I'd keep bantams. Always wanted to keep bantams.'

'What's bantams?'

'Hens. Small ones. Five or six. Then it'd be fresh eggs for breakfast every day.'

I watched an oldish person, perhaps she was a granny, but not as old as the one with the chopsticks, taking off a toddler's nappy and leading him, quite bare except for his sun hat, to splash in the water. He picked up pine cones that were floating in the sea and handed them to the old woman to put in her pockets.

'D'you want to know something, Bob?' I said.

'Tell me.'

'I haven't wet the bed, not once, since we left.'

I thought he might say something like, 'Well done

that man!' He didn't. I had to push for any sign of approval. 'Bit amazing, isn't it?' I said.

He turned on me, suddenly irritable. 'D'you want the honest answer? Because if so, it's, "No! Pissing the bed's hardly something to be proud of." '

I said, 'I'm not proud. I just thought you'd be pleased to hear I seem to have stopped.'

He said, 'OK. I am pleased. And you've done better than me. I went on till I got my first girlfriend when I was seventeen.'

'*You?*' There were obviously things I didn't know about him.

He said, quietly as though he thought the old couple with the chopsticks might be listening in, 'You're not the only one, you know.'

'Only what?'

'I grew up in care, too. Blackrock House, it was called. Nobody wanted me, either. They said I was nothing but a nit-carrier.'

'What's a nit-carrier?'

'Just use your imagination. They kept my head shaved on a number one all the years I was in care. Maybe it's a cool way to be now but back then, no way. It marked me out. Everybody could see I was a no-hoper from the Home. That's why I kept the rat. I wasn't going to let anyone tell me how to wear my hair.'

I was so surprised I didn't know what to say. I chucked a flat stone on to the water and tried to make it skim. But the surface wasn't smooth enough.

He said, 'And inside, too. I was just the same as you.'

I thought, Bet you weren't. I said, 'Did you nick things?'

'From time to time.'

'Did you lie?'

'All the time.'

'Did you cheat on your pals?'

'Yes.'

'Did you hit people who didn't deserve it?'

'No, I never did that. Do you do that?'

I was going to say 'No' but that wouldn't have been entirely true. So I said, 'Well, I used to.'

He said, 'If we're going to stick together, you'll have to give that up.'

'I'll try.' If we were a pair of no-hoper kids from care trying to make a life together, we'd have to trust each other all the way and beyond.

We were in the southern hemisphere, so the sun was moving across the sky in the north. Things here might be back-to-front but not upside down. Bob's nose and ears were very red but he and I were both definitely the right way up. We shifted ourselves to some deeper shade at the foot of a dark-red cliff. We sat on a red rock. I threw pebbles into the sea. Bob said we ought to start making plans, only he called it 'taking stock of the situation'.

'OK,' I said.

He said, 'So what've we got? Between us?'

He emptied his pockets. He'd got the two passports, travellers' cheques that could be turned into nearly any currency in the whole world, some airline vouchers to compensate for our misdirected baggage, two round-the-world tickets, half used, a clean handkerchief, and a pair of nail clippers.

'Oh,' he said, inspecting them. 'Carrying dangerous goods. Dunno why I brought them along. Still, may come in useful some day.'

I went through my bum-bag. There wasn't a lot, but it was more than Bob.

I had a toy 747, which Bob wasn't interested in so I gave it to a girl with a plastic bucket hunting for driftwood along the rocks. I also had a crumpled map of Hong Kong.

'Might prove useful,' Bob said, 'if we get hold of a boat some day and decide to sail back to the old country.'

I also had a sachet of lemon shampoo from the Via Appia Antica Hotel, a pack of coloured pencils, one spare sock but not the other, a plastic fork and spoon, salt, pepper and mustard in a sealed pack from our last flight, and the school notebook.

We set out our possessions on the rock for inspection.

'Great,' said Bob. 'That's more than enough to start with.'

I said, 'We'll need to buy essential stuff, won't we? Toothbrushes, soap.' I added, 'And maybe a surfboard and some roller-blades and a pair of sunglasses.' Already I could see myself speeding up and down the Corso on my new roller-blades, wearing my new wraparound sunnies. And we'd need to get some better clothes for him.

'You'd look a cool dude in one of those Hawaiian shirts. You know, with the big coloured flowers all over.'

He gave his fat belly a scratch.

'OK. If you insist. But first we'll need to find a place to crash tonight. Backpackers' hostel? We'd save on the cash.'

Sounded all right to me.

He said, 'And we'll need to find you a place in school.'

'Hey, steady on.'

'We will find a school and you will go to it. Not sometimes. Every day. I'll find a job and I'll go to it. Every day. That'll be the deal.'

Reluctantly, I agreed to spit and shake on it. I thought, even if I had to go to school, there'd be the evenings to speed along the Corso on my blades and the weekends to learn to surf.

We walked the length of the beach, and reached another one beyond. And another beyond that. We could hear the big rollers booming out in the sea as they crashed on to the reef. Red-beaked gulls trotted along the sand in front of us as though showing us the way.

'Dad,' I said. I don't know how that slipped out. But it did.

'Yes?'

'I'm getting ever so hungry. Could we go and find a place to eat?'

'OK, sport. Time for tucker,' he said and gave me a big wink. 'Shark steaks and fries suit you?'

'Beaut.'

BLACKTHORN, WHITETHORN

Rachel Anderson

It's all change in our family. Everything's gone – house, car, furniture – the end of our old life. And all because Dad got himself in a money muddle. He's burying his shame – and us.

So now it's just this ugly bungalow, among ruined cottages, muddy sugarbeet fields and nettles. No shops, no street lights, no phone box . . .

It's dead and it's lonely.

That is, until Ada and Lily let me enter their lives – and their memories. Then everything begins to come alive . . .